the
Kiss of
the Prison
Dancer

Jerome Richard

etchings by Tom Sherwood

the permanent press
sag harbor, new york 11963

Copyright© 2004 by Jerome Richard

Library of Congress Cataloging-in-Publication Data

Richard, Jerome, 1931-
    The kiss of the prison dancer : a novel / by Jerome Richard.
    p. cm.
    ISBN 1-57962-102-3 (alk. paper)
    1. San Francisco (Calif.)--Fiction. 2. Concentration Camp
inmates--Fiction. 3. Holocaust survivors--Fiction 4. Trials
(Murder)--Fiction. 5. Neo-Nazis--Fiction. 6. Witnesses--
Fiction. 7. Germany--Fiction. I. Title.

PS3618.I334K57 2004
813'.6—dc22

2003065553

Printed in The United States of America

THE PERMANENT PRESS
4170 Noyac Road
Sag Harbor, NY 11963

For Michael and David

For their encouragement and advice, I would like to thank Priscilla, Sandra, Tom, Judith and Martin Shepard, and especially my indispensible wife Carolyn.

The boy hesitated and then ran....

1

Max put on his tie because he believed that people who were well-dressed encountered less trouble in the world. He was only going for a walk in Golden Gate Park, but the newspapers told of hoodlums who hid near the dark walks and beat people up just for the thrill of beating them up, and only last month there had been a murder. His eyes were the only parts of his body that were tired. Perhaps when he got back, he thought, he would be able to fall asleep.

Squinting through the frameless hexagons of his glasses, he adjusted the tie and then turned quickly away from the mirror. He was fifty-nine, and he knew too well what his face looked like: tiny red streams feeding the brown lakes of his pupils, dark brown hair salted white that edged back from his forehead like snow in March, ending in a small tide of waves at his neck. He also knew the bone structure behind the face, had seen it with the skin stretched tight as old leather and two craters where his eyes should be. He even knew the face behind that one, the face of the university student with dark wavy hair slicked back and parted in the middle, and eyes that were quick and bright.

Leaving the room was always difficult. First he faced the door and listened for footsteps, then he put on his jacket and his raincoat and checked the clock. It was just after midnight. He turned the page on his desk calendar and June 4, 1977 stared blankly at him.

In the street Max took a deep breath, pulling it in through his nose. The air was lightly seasoned with ocean, but there was not the sinus-closing fog that got inside his head and chilled his nerves. There were two ways into the park, a tunnel near where he stood and an open path a few blocks away. He stared at the dead eye of the tunnel and then started for the path. Before he went very far, a young couple came through the tunnel, laughing and holding hands. Max decided the tunnel was safe. "Good evening," he said as he passed them.

The tunnel went under the park road. He crossed back over the road and sat on a bench in front of a little grove. A car appeared around the far turn. When it slowed up in front of where he sat, he moved to the edge of the bench, as far out of the pool of light as he could get. Then he saw that the driver was a woman and had only stopped because of the lone lamppost that hung over the road. He watched her examine something, a map perhaps or a paper with directions written on it, and then scan the road in both directions. He wondered if he should offer to help and was about to get up when she drove off. Max watched the car until it disappeared around a curve. It often annoyed him that the lights stretched out over the road but there were none over the benches. He looked up. The twisted limbs of a tree, like the old hag of children's stories, reached out over the bench. "Suppose someone wanted to read?" he asked the old hag.

He would rather have come to the park during the day, but on weekends it was crowded and crowds made him nervous, and weekdays he worked. His job consisted mainly of filing papers for a charitable organization. He knew that the job itself was charity; he would leave it if there were anything else he could do, but they never even let him finish college so now he spent his days taking papers from a basket and feeding them to a filing cabinet. *The keeper of the filing cabinet*, he thought, leaning against the back of the bench and listening to the rustle of leaves and the hum of the occasional car. He wanted to be a teacher, a professor of German literature. He laughed. Herr Professor Max Friedman. German literature. He laughed again. "Can't you see me?" he asked the hag. As if in response there was a noise in the grove behind him and Max jumped up, his heart leaping against his ribs. A bird, he assured himself, or a rabbit.

Max stepped out on the path and looked around. Only the mad shapes of trees stood between him and the broad avenue outside the park. He listened and could feel his ears prickle as he strained the faint rustle of leaves for other sounds. Now he decided to walk the other way, to the next entrance. Behind him there was a rushing noise and he whirled, but it was only a car on the road. Its headlights blinded Max for a moment, and then it glided peacefully by. Max shook his head at his own foolishness. A little walk, he decided, was just what he needed to tire himself out enough to get to sleep. Otherwise, this would be one of those nights when he lay awake until just before the alarm went off. Once he woke up in the office to find the cleaning lady scrubbing the floors and the windows dark with night and he did not speak to anyone for a week because they did not wake him up. "Suppose I had an important appointment?" he said.

He picked his way along the path, letting his mind wander back to the days long ago when he walked with Sarah through the Tiergarten in Berlin. He remembered the first time she slipped her hand into his and how sometimes while they walked they would recite poetry to each other. He would memorize a poem before he called on her, saying it over and over in his head as they walked to the park, and then-.

Suddenly there was a noise in the bushes beside him.

Max held his breath. Someone leaped out and landed on the path in front of him, a young man, a boy, poised momentarily with his arms outspread like a bird winged and motionless for just the shadow of a second. Max and the young man exchanged looks, not of surprise so much as incredulity, each of them facing a ghost, before the young man turned, the bird finding the wind, and ran off down the path. Max could still see his face, as if he had left it there when he ran, blond hair on a football with deep, scared eyes and a cupid mouth open as if to talk or scream, a boy seventeen or eighteen, pimples. Then the face vanished too and Max started to breathe again. Another noise came from the bushes. It sounded like someone clearing his throat and Max took it as a warning, thinking that whoever had scared the boy was still in there, and he hurried down the path.

Far ahead he saw the boy appear in the light of the next streetlamp. He turned and threw something, but it hit a tree and bounced back into the path. The boy hesitated and then ran, disappearing suddenly like some magician's bird. That's where the exit must be, Max thought, but he had run as far as he could and he had to stop to catch his breath. He looked back. He had only gone twenty yards but no one was coming so he looked ahead to see what the boy had thrown. Max walked as quickly as he could, ran a few paces, then walked some more. He stooped down and picked up a small stone, wondering why the boy threw it away, or carried it at all, but when he looked closer he saw that it was not a stone, it was a button, a fancy one with a raised design. He put it in his pocket and ran again until he came to the Park exit.

There was no one there. A few cars were all the movement in the street. Max leaned against the bus stop and breathed deeply. Perhaps it was just a game, he thought.

Maybe the boy was playing hide and-seek with his friends and I scared him. He walked home, not feeling any more sleepy than he had an hour earlier.

Max rented a room from a retired couple named Thompson whose only son worked for an oil company in Venezuela. When he first came to San Francisco he rented an apartment near the foot of Nob Hill, but when he looked out his window all he could see were the houses across the street and when he lay in bed at night he could hear the footsteps of people going to other apartments in the building. There was a nice little park on top of the hill. He liked to sit there and look out over the city which, from that height, resembled cities in the Middle East, but his legs resisted the climb and it embarrassed him to be seen leaning against one of the fancy buildings towards the top of the hill, resting and working his lungs like a leaky bellows. Down the hill there was nothing but cheap bars and nightclubs, too shoddy to walk through during the day and too noisy to live near at night, so one day he answered an ad and moved into a large room upstairs in one of the houses that stand shoulder to shoulder in the Richmond district out near the park. From that room he could see the sky, even when he lay in bed. He did that a lot: lie in bed and look at the sky. It didn't matter if the sun was shining or if rain fell like God's tears on his window.

At first Max thought he would have someone to talk to in the old couple and they must have too, but Max wanted to talk about books and they only wanted to discuss what they read in the newspaper or saw on television. Even when they asked him about Europe it was only so they could tell him about their son in Venezuela. But Max didn't want to talk about Europe and he didn't care about Venezuela or their son, even if he was living in what they still called his room. So he spent his time reading and tak-

9

ing long, slow walks, going straight to his room again when he returned, and only stopping to chat and sometimes watch television with them at the beginning of the month when he paid his rent.

They were sitting in front of the television set when he came in and Max realized it was not yet one o'clock because they always watched the late show which was over at one before they went to bed. Max thought he had been gone for hours. He did not bother to say hello, he seldom did, but Mrs. Thompson turned around and waved to him. He went upstairs and lay down to see if sleep would come. If he felt it coming, he would get undressed.

It was a large room and the bed in it was meant for two. He sometimes wondered if they got it after their son moved out or if he actually slept in such a big bed himself. He didn't like it and wanted to ask for a narrower one, but he didn't know how to explain it.

One corner of the room was provided with a stove and a small refrigerator. He called it his kitchen. If sleep did not come, he would warm some milk and take it back to bed with him. He closed his eyes and saw again the frightened face of the boy in the park and how the boy ran and all the running he had seen in his life. And then he was aware that something was different. In the past, even in America, whenever he saw someone run he expected to hear gunshots. Even when someone ran for a bus, even in a movie- he remembered one he saw not long ago where there was a track meet and as the athletes with the big numbers sewn on the backs of their undershirts burst from their blocks, Max was certain the starter would turn his pistol on them- running meant that gunshots were sure to follow. But not tonight. The boy ran down the park path and Max heard nothing but his footsteps. That was something. He looked at the blue numbers on his forearm and wondered if those would ever go away.

Angry with himself for thinking about the numbers, he got up and splashed milk in the pan, spilling a little of it on the floor. He mopped it up while the milk in the pan warmed and then he poured it into a glass and took it to bed where he settled down with the warm milk and a book. He didn't like warm milk. He read until the milk cooled and then he drank it down in three gulps and got up to brush his teeth and cross the date off on the calendar.

Later, he dreamed he was in a forest. He could hear the beating of drums and a great white bird kept fluttering to the ground in front of him and taking off again, leading Max deeper into the woods. He wanted to go back. Through the dream came the thin high sound of a siren. Max turned over, but he did not wake up.

2

At work the next morning, Max hummed to himself a German lullaby while he waited for the mail that would give him something to do. Another man worked in the room with Max, also a refugee. His name was Shmuel and his job was to open the mail, passing the appropriate letters to Max. He also sent out the applications and in between he carried folders to whoever needed them. Shmuel sang wordless songs to himself while he worked, but he sang them out loud though Max had often asked him not to. Sometimes Max hummed louder when Shmuel sang until it sounded as if a Chassidic cantor had been captured by a swarm of bees. Shmuel had another habit that annoyed Max: he would get to know which cases specially interested him and when a letter came about that case he

11

would shout out and bring it over all by itself like the next installment of a novel. Max waited, hummed, and kept one eye on Shmuel. Sure enough: "Hooray," cried Shmuel, "another letter from Mrs. Greenberg." He waved the letter in the air. "Bring it with the rest of the mail," Max said, but it was no use. Shmuel slid his letter opener through the envelope and brought Mrs. Greenberg's letter over to Max.

"Put it down already," Max said.

Shmuel put the letter in the tray on Max's desk. Then Max took the letter out and began to read it. Shmuel looked over his shoulder.

"This is my job, Shmuel, thank you. The letter is confidential."

"I'm not a gossip columnist."

"You're not supposed to read the clients' letters." But Max held it up where Shmuel could see it. Once he refused to let Shmuel read a letter and Shmuel sulked all morning and did not open the rest of the mail.

Shmuel expressed sympathy between his teeth. "That poor woman," he said, going back to his desk.

Mrs. Greenberg's husband had disappeared three years ago; now another man wanted to marry her and this had brought her to the agency for advice. Max had seen several such cases in the last ten years, but this one had suddenly become interesting when Mr. Greenberg showed up again. He had established a good business in Mexico and Mrs. Greenberg was writing to say that he wanted her to go to Mexico with him and she would like to go but she thinks she is pregnant by the second man, could she come in for advice. If she were his client, Max thought, he would tell her to sleep quick with the husband and then tell him it was his child. But she was not his client. Max took Mrs. Greenberg's folder out of the file, put the letter in it, and put the folder in the box for Shmuel to take to Dr. Resnick. Resnick would advise her to tell everything to the husband right away and if he really loved her he would still take her back to Mexico with him. Advice like that Max could write her on a postcard. He wondered why he didn't become a psychiatrist.

When Shmuel brought the rest of the mail, Max quickly thumbed through the letters and applications and saw that it would not be easy to make the work last until five o'clock. When he first came to the agency he worked quickly, often finishing before it was time to go home, but when he asked the director of the agency for more work, he was told there was nothing else and the director looked disappointed, so Max learned to make the papers last until five o'clock each day. He made one pile of the letters that required answers and another of the applications and letters that went into folders. While he worked at this Shmuel read the newspaper; he would have nothing to do until Max gave him the day's folders to distribute.

"I see you had a little excitement out your way last night," Shmuel called across the room.

"What excitement?"

Shmuel came across the room with the newspaper, his short legs going very fast as they always did and his back slightly bent, as if he were riding a bicycle, and spread it out on Max's desk. Max had noticed the headline earlier on the bus, but the person who was sitting next to him turned the page and all Max saw was something about a murder. Now he saw that a girl had been raped and killed in Golden Gate Park. A man out walking his dog late at night had found the body, or rather his dog had. The girl was seventeen; she had been raped and then her neck slit with the jagged edge of a broken beer bottle. There was a picture of the girl's body covered with a sheet lying in a small grove which the caption said was not far from the park entrance on Tenth Street.

"Terrible," Max said.

"You didn't know?"

"No," Max said.

Shmuel left the paper with him, picked up the folders, and started on his rounds. Max glanced at the story again, but did not read it. Stories like that depressed him. He only remembered that he had been in the park last night and that there had been someone in the bushes, maybe even the murderer, and he was glad that nothing happened to him. Poor girl, he thought, putting the newspaper aside and picking up a letter from a woman who wanted to know if the agency could help her find her son who had run away from home.

Shmuel returned just before twelve and took out a cream cheese and lox sandwich and a small jar of pickled herring. Max waited until the hour and then he went to the luncheonette around the corner and ordered a toasted cheese sandwich and a malted. They didn't actually make malteds. No one did anymore and they told Max that several times. They only made milk shakes without the malt that had become too expensive. Max understood. He drank the milk shakes, but he kept calling them malteds out of habit. Someone left the newspaper on the table and Max was looking at the picture again, trying to place the grove, when the waitress came with his order. She looked over his shoulder at the story. "A maniac," she said. "One of those sex maniacs. You're not safe anywhere."

"They were in the park," Max told her.

"I'd like to catch the guy that did it," the waitress said. "I'd strangle him with my bare hands."

She was a big, blond woman. Max looked at her hands. He wanted to tell her that he lived near the park, but

14

she turned away to greet a new customer. He studied the picture again, the hand sticking out from under the sheet, and then his eye caught the shape of the sheet as it humped over her legs which were still spread and he turned to the editorial page.

The afternoon crept across his desk in a procession of papers, but every time he stopped working he saw again the grove with the girl's body lying sprawled and sheet covered on the grass and as the afternoon wore on the grove seemed more and more familiar.

"You're not taking a break?" Shmuel asked at three o'clock.

"I want to finish early today. I have an appointment."

Shmuel took a thermos of tea out of his desk. "A woman?" he asked.

Max went on working, but he could not get his mind off the scene in the newspaper photograph, a scene he increasingly saw colliding with another scene, a young man with terror in his eyes leaping from the bushes, the two scenes coming together like two trains on the same track, though he tried to keep them apart. A little before five o'clock, he put on his hat and coat and hurried past Shmuel and out of the office. The receptionist said goodnight, but he only waved a hand at her as, head down, he pushed through the doors and out into the street.

The agency occupied what had once been a private house; only the sign outside distinguished it from neighboring houses. Max was glad he did not work downtown where crowds of people swept blindly along the gaudy streets and the rush hour buses were packed like cattle cars. Here in a neighborhood of stucco houses with gabled roofs Max could come to work and leave as if he were visiting a friend and ride a nearly empty bus well ahead of the tide that was gathering downtown. Children played in the streets and housewives hurried home with the day's shopping clutched to their breasts. Some wheeled the groceries along like infants in little carts while the actual infants ran along behind, crying because they had been displaced. Sometimes Max would sniff the air and be rewarded with the odor of chicken roasting or even, from one particular house, and there only on Friday evenings, the rich, thick smell of baking bread. Usually he enjoyed walking the two blocks to the bus and he took his time, watching the children play or deliberating about his dinner, but this time he burst into the street and hurried away while children stared after him as if a fish had leaped from the water. He had to know if last night he had stood outside the grove in which the girl was killed.

The bus took Max to the green lace wall of the park. He got off and watched the bus proceed into the park, but he did not go in. *Suppose it is the same place*, he thought, *what is it my business?* He walked back and forth a little on the sidewalk. Traffic was picking up and there was a loud honking of horns as someone failed to respond to a green light. Other people were going into the park, perhaps to see where the crime had been committed. Max said to himself, *Why look for trouble?* And then, as often happened, another voice sounded in his mind and started talking to the first and Max stood on the sidewalk and listened.

Suppose the boy is in there?

And the first voice said, Suppose he is? So what?

So what! The criminal always returns to the scene of the crime!

"You getting on or aren't you?" A bus had pulled up and the driver yelled at Max.

Max shook his head and moved away from the bus stop. Then he was moving away from the park too, crossing the street and going home. He could picture the boy, could see every detail of his face, the blue eyes, the blond hair, the pimples, the fear that ripped his mouth open and narrowed his eyes. That boy was not a murderer. He was scared, Max told himself, scared. Probably he went into the bushes looking for something and he found the body and got scared just like anyone and he ran away. "Just a boy," he said out loud, and the silent voices agreed.

At the door to the house, Max had an idea. Instead of eating at home, he would treat himself to dinner at the Russian restaurant on Geary Boulevard. Eating out was something he ordinarily did only on Sundays when he spent the day at the beach or the zoo and could not bear his own room after all that space, or else he celebrated his birthday by eating at the Jewish restaurant downtown, but he could not face his room tonight and anyway he felt somehow that he had earned a dinner out. Besides, he thought, how do I know it's even the same grove?

He ordered borsht and, though he knew he should not have fried foods, piroshkes, and finally, after some hesitation, an éclair to go with his tea and then he sat back and wondered why he let himself eat these things as fingers of acid began to claw at his heart. He drank two glasses of water, but it didn't help and when he left the restaurant fog was creeping over the city and Max knew his sinuses would close and he would have a headache. The lights of the stores on Geary Boulevard melted in the fog and people walked ghost- like, shifting gray shapes that loomed out of the mist and disappeared again. Max buttoned his coat up to the collar. He found the corner drugstore and bought a roll of stomach mints and then he hurried home.

Sleep was the only release Max ever found from the pain of a sinus headache, but the old couple were watching television when he came in and Max heard the

17

announcer say: "Police report no clues yet in last night's brutal rape and murder of seventeen-year-old Linda Jordan." Max put one foot on the stairs to his room. "Hello, Mr. Friedman," the old woman called. "Shush," her husband whispered. Max went into the living room. The picture of the grove was on the television screen though the body was no longer there.

The old woman motioned him to a seat and said, "Isn't it awful? If they catch whoever did it, they ought to shoot him."

"I've got a better idea," the old man cackled, as the picture changed and the announcer began the commercial. "Something more appropriate."

His wife turned to him with a look that warned him to stop, but he swished his hand through the air with a cutting motion and then laughed and slapped his thighs. Max took another mint.

Now Max felt trapped. He didn't want to see the rest of the news or sit there in that gloomy room, but he couldn't jump up and leave. The room depressed him; china animals were everywhere, a large cocker spaniel slept on the television set, a deer stood on green china grass on the coffee table, over the bureau hung a plastic tree, its branches sporting tiny china birds, and worst of all, next to Mrs. Thompson sat a life size china cat, its pale green eyes fixed forever on the television set, its mouth cast in an eternal smile. The Thompsons collected china animals; more were scattered about the house and one sat in his room, a giraffe with a tree on a green china oasis that he was afraid to put away because he did not want to offend the Thompsons.

"I wouldn't go in that park at night for all the money in the world," the old woman said.

"Mr. Friedman goes all the time," the old man replied.

18

He saw that Mrs. Thompson was watching him, waiting for him to say something. "I don't go there all the time," Max said. "To tell you the truth, I'm afraid of going there when it's dark too." He wanted to tell them it was none of their business, but he could see that their minds were working now. He smiled to show the old woman that he shared her fears of the park.

"But you do go?" she asked.

Should I deny it? Max considered. They both turned to face him now, the television announcer spoke to their backs. What if the old man follows me? "Well, I was there last night, but that was the first time in a long time."

"Were you near where it happened? I mean, did you"

"No," Max said. "I didn't see anything." And he excused himself, complaining of his headache.

"I hope they catch him," the old woman said.

"Me too."

The old man made the cutting motion in the air and winked at Max who hurried upstairs.

His room was cold. Max locked the door and put the electric heater on. He put the milk on to warm while he undressed and then he drank it still warm and threw himself on the bed and tried to sleep.

3

Max awoke the next morning with a thin film of sweat coating his body. No light showed at the window and when he looked at the clock he saw that it was still an hour until the alarm would ring. He turned the pillow over and pulled his pajamas away from his sweating chest and then lay face up, staring at the ceiling. A strange feeling spread from his heart to every corner of his body and he lay without moving even a finger. He knew the feeling, just as he recognized the terrible silence that had seized the room. It was the feeling one got in the camps when someone had escaped during the night, the same sensation the prisoner must have felt as he crawled through his tunnel or slipped through the barbed wire: The silence was the vacuum between the prisoner's leaving and the arrival in the morning of the Kommandant. Everyone knew when there had been an escape, the silence spread from the missing man's barracks to every barracks in the camp and there was nothing to do but wait for the Kommandant to come and see what new reprisals he had invented. But when one knew how the prisoner had managed his escape, then one woke up an hour before the rest and stared at the ceiling. Max never knew how he survived the camps: He supposed it was because he didn't really care, not since the day he learned that his wife had been killed, or as the Sonderkommando had put it, was *den Schornstein hinauf.* For a while he hated the old grimacing Jew who had given him the news, but then he did not see him around any more and he knew he had gone where his wife had gone and he stopped hating him. Then he would stand at the double row of barbed wire and stare out at the peaceful plains of the German countryside and there was nothing left to hate. He worked in the munitions factory because they told him to and once he stole a pair of pliers from the factory and slipped it to another prisoner in exchange for a piece of bread, lying in bed the next morning staring at the ceiling not so much for himself, though he knew what they did to anyone aiding in an escape, but for the prisoner looking desperately for a place to hide on the peaceful plain.

Now he lay on a bed in an upstairs bedroom in San Francisco waiting for the alarm to ring as he had once waited for the Allied troops to free him. The prisoners weren't even sure if they would be Russian or American or British troops, though the sounds of the big guns had come from the west and someone said that would mean either British or Americans. Max was in the hospital when they came. He was lucky. They were American troops and they arrived just in time to interrupt a slaughter of the camp's survivors. He remembered the American soldiers coming into the barracks the Germans had called a hospital and how quietly they went from bed to bed, as if the prisoners might be sleeping. He remembered that one of the soldiers cried and another vomited.

Afterwards he went to Israel, but there was nothing for him to do there. He applied to the university, but he did not have his degree and anyway they had enough teachers of German literature, so he learned Hebrew and got a job as a translator at one of the resettlement agencies, but the young Israelis did not talk to him and the old survivors talked only about the camps, comparing conditions and asking over and over if he had seen their wife or sister or brother, so one day he decided to resettle himself again and he came to America. He lay in bed remembering it all until the alarm rang and he jumped as if he had been asleep. At first he thought he had been dreaming, but then he knew he was not dreaming and he was surprised because he had not thought about the camp for a long time. He had died back there in the camp, probably on the day he learned about his wife. Gradually he stopped talking to his friends and after a while his friends stopped calling him Professor, and then he had no friends and he went through the daily routine because there was nothing else for a dead man to do. So he was surprised to find he could think about it at all, though he knew that night in the park that he was coming back to life because he was afraid.

He was brushing his teeth when he remembered that. He had almost forgotten what happened in the park. The thing to do was to go to the police and tell them about the boy; if he is innocent the police will know, or at least they will find out. But then he remembered the old man's obscene gesture and he shuddered, and that made him think of the waitress with the big hands who talked of strangling. A voice in him whispered, *Suppose he's guilty?* And another voice answered, He's just a boy, how could he be guilty? Max looked out the window. The city was choking on fog; in the street, people disappeared in it, the whole city disappeared in it, leaving only the bush and the thin row of red carnations that the old man had planted in front of the house, and a small piece of sidewalk not yet engulfed. The boy and the murdered girl seemed to disappear like the park itself in the fog. Max pulled down the shade. *Why should I get involved?* he thought. *It's not my business.*

He made coffee, but he found his hand trembling and when he raised the cup the coffee spilled. He tried holding the cup with both hands and that way he got the cup to his lips and sipped it. He became angry with the cup, with

22

Das geht mich nichts an

his hands. They seemed to conspire against him and when he held the cup out in front of him, still holding it with both hands, it dropped, hitting the saucer and carrying that to the ground with it where cup and saucer both broke and Max watched the hot coffee spread on his lap and said over and over to himself: *Das geht mich nichts an!*

Das geht mich nichts an! The words spun round in his head and when he said it aloud they came out in English, but his eyes were wet with tears. "It's none of my business." He still remembered the first time he said it, after the first political arrests when his father read the story in the newspaper and asked what he thought about it and he said they were communists who were arrested and it was none of his business. Then it was Jehovah's Witnesses and it was even less his business. By the time the first Jews were arrested and taken to the camps he was going with Sarah and she flung the paper at him, saying, "Is it still none of your business, Max?" He said, "Yes, Sarah. That's right. It's none of my business." Only then he started to hear it all over the city, in the streets, the streetcars, even in the university, long past the time he realized it was his business and it was too late to say so. He wondered what the neighbors said the day he and Sarah were arrested. *Das gehen unseren nichts an?*

Max sighed deeply and wiped his eyes. For another minute he stared at his coffee soaked pants and wondered whether to wipe them off first or dry his own wet legs. Finally, he shrugged and got up, taking off his pants and limping to the nearest towel. He dried himself and then tried to wash off the coffee stains, giving up after he could no longer tell the coffee from the water and hanging the pants up to dry and be taken to the cleaners. It occurred to him to try the radio for news and he put it on and listened while he put on a new pair of pants and cleaned up the broken cup and saucer but it was too early for news, or too late, and he was going to be late for work.

Shmuel was already there reading the paper when Max came in.

"Anything new?" Max asked.

"New?" Shmuel glanced around the office and then at Max. "What could be new?" he said at last.

He wasn't even trying to be funny, Max realized. "I mean the murder, the rape in the park. They caught him?"

Shmuel turned the pages of the newspaper; he reached the editorial page before he answered. "I don't see anything."

During the morning break, Max usually read, but this morning he argued with himself about calling the police. Once he even picked up the receiver, but he saw Shmuel watching him and he put it down. The boy was innocent, he told himself, and anyway the police must know all about him by now. But in the luncheonette that noon he began to wonder if it hadn't all been a dream because no one spoke about it. In the booth behind him two men talked about baseball and at the cash register a woman argued about the price of a hamburger. Even the waitress, the one with the big hands, said nothing when she took his order, and when she brought the sandwich and the milk shake she only smiled and said something about the weather. Even her hands looked smaller. So when on his way home that evening he saw a newspaper headline that said: SUSPECT ARRESTED IN PARK MURDER, he thought, *Oh, No!* because he was almost convinced that it had been a dream, a mistake.

He put his money down on the counter and stared at the top half of the paper with its thick black headline. He did not want to turn it over, did not want to see the boy's face. Someone else came to buy a paper and Max had to pick his up from the counter and move away from the stand. Still he held the top half of the paper towards him. He closed his eyes and the boy's face swam towards him, pleading, asking for help. Max closed his eyes. He heard the bus drive up and the people getting on and off while he turned the paper over. When he opened his eye he was looking at a picture of someone with dark hair and a mous-tache and pushed in- eyes. Max tore the page finding the story. This was the one they had arrested, this was the sus-pect: There was no picture of a blond haired boy with pim-ples. Police said they were sure this was their man; they had witnesses who had seen him in the park that night, other witnesses who had seen him with the girl, even the girl's father knew him, had told him to stay away from his daughter. His name was Mortimer Holtz. Max felt grateful to him: He didn't look anything like the boy Max had seen in the park.

"It wasn't the boy," he said to an old man standing on the corner.

"What bus did you say?" the old man asked.

Max hurried up the street to the next stop

4

On Saturday Holtz said he was innocent. When Max heard that on the radio he became very angry. He was eat-ing breakfast at the time and he could not finish it, dump-ing the coffee down the sink and later cutting himself when he shaved so that he had to wear a bit of toilet paper on his chin for an hour and could not go out, pacing his room and anxious to get a newspaper. He calmed down by the time he stopped bleeding, telling himself that of course

Holtz would say he was innocent, what else could he do. Still, Max walked very fast, even ran across the intersection, to get the paper which he read in the street.

The paper was reassuring. Holtz said he was innocent, but a detective was quoted as saying, "This is the man. I've never been surer of anything in my career." They had learned that the girl had tried to break off seeing him and so anyone could see that Holtz had a motive. There were also more details about Holtz's life. He had gone to college but had not done well and he quit after the first year. One of his professors remembered him as arrogant. That's good, Max thought; he read that line over. Holtz had been working as a shoe salesman when he was arrested and his employer said he had a good record there. His parents were separated when he was young. No one knew where his father was; his mother died three years ago at which time Holtz came to San Francisco from the small town in Arizona where he had been brought up. An orphan, Max thought.

He took a book to the park and he stayed there even though a wind came up and his hands shivered with the cold, but he could not read. Why do I want this Holtz to be the killer instead of the boy? he wondered. As if the boy's blood were redder than the orphan's. He wished that no one killed the girl. Or that she killed herself. (*And raped herself too?* a voice in his head demanded.) He wished that he had not gone to the park that night and then he would not even be thinking about it because ordinarily he did not even read the crime stories in the paper.

His whole body began to shake with the cold until he had to go home. On the way he stopped to see what was playing at the local theater. It was a musical and he didn't like musicals, but that night he went anyway.

Sunday looked like it would be a nice day. He turned

the radio on to get some news and the weather report, but all he got were music and church services. He started breakfast and on the hour he tried the radio again. The news was sensational. Out of the jumble of noises Max heard as he worked the dial back and forth one word leaped out at him: "Nazi!" He twisted the dial back through the hymns and commercials until he captured the right voice again: It was just describing a picture police had found of a group of men wearing uniforms with swastika armbands. Holtz was in the picture. The announcer went on to other news, but after trying a few more stations, Max went out to get a newspaper.

Downstairs, Max met Mr. Thompson working on the rose bush in front of the house.

"Did you hear?" Max asked him.

"Where? What?" the old man responded, looking around.

"Never mind. Good morning."

The old man nodded and Max walked very quickly until he was out of sight and then ran a little until he was on Geary Boulevard where he bought a newspaper. It was true. The headline said: MURDER SUSPECT A NAZI, and there was the picture the announcer had talked about, a row of young men wearing uniforms with boots and armbands and in front of them an older man wearing the same uniform but with a cap on his head and a Sam Browne belt across his chest and his arms planted on his hips as if defying the photographer to capture him on film. And there was Holtz standing in the row, second from the right according to the caption. Max juggled the bulky Sunday paper to read the story. Police said they suspected Holtz of being a member of the organization when they arrested him, but that he denied it until they discovered the picture, cut out of a newspaper, when they searched his

28

room.The picture was taken at a rally held in Union Square about a year ago; the rally ended in a riot and police said they had kept watch over the group ever since. They held maneuvers in the hills south of San Francisco and they picketed several speakers in the past year. Police said as far as they knew the murdered girl was not connected with the organization.

Max hurried home. When he got to his room he read the story in the magazine section where the news of the week was reviewed. It told again how the girl was discovered and how detectives quickly closed in on Holtz, but the story about Holtz being a Nazi wasn't included, that was in the main news on page one and Max read that story again. A Nazi, he told himself, and laughed. He read the story for the third time, spit on the picture, and then, believing he had met justice, Max went to the park, whistling a German hiking song.

It was not yet noon, but already the grass was patched with blankets bearing couples or families, their children skipping between the islands of food. The walks too were filling with people and Max picked his way among them like a mushroom gatherer in a forest of unfamiliar plants. Crowds reminded him of Germany and the camp. Even in the bus on the way to work he would sometimes feel his heart beat faster, especially when the driver asked everyone to move to the back and he was swept along in the mass of obliging people. When the man sitting next to him had not bathed or used his deodorant liberally enough, Max would move near an open window if he could. Now he ducked out of the crowd and into the aquarium where he had never been before.

The aquarium too was crowded and Max pushed along, smelling the ocean and thinking of Sarah, wishing she were there so he could tell her about Holtz being a

Nazi. He felt so old without her. The voices of the crowd echoing off the tile walls reminded him of the Berlin subway and he could almost feel her hand as they ran for a train and tried not to lose each other in the rush of people. He pushed through the crowd in the aquarium hall and found himself facing an ugly black creature resting on the sand at the bottom of a tank. It was a lungfish, a living fossil, the sign said. Max stared at it a long time. "How did we survive?" he asked it.

The benches at the music concourse were nearly empty. Max took a seat and stared at the stage. No one appeared in the band shell. In the row in front of Max a man with a knotted handkerchief on his head slumped in his seat and snored and farther down Max's row a fat woman with butcher-shop arms busily pulled sandwiches and hardboiled eggs and fruit from a paper bag and spread them on the seats around her. She reminded him of a waitress in a café the students patronized. One of his friends told him she was a whore and Max had sexual fantasies in which he saw himself rolling in her arms. Looking at this older reproduction of the waitress it occurred to Max that the sins of the flesh were as nothing compared to the sins of the imagination. The fat woman smiled at him over a hardboiled egg and Max got up and began to walk. He stopped as he often did before the statue of Goethe and Schiller and briefly bowed his head.

At the lake he bought a frankfurter and a cup of coffee and went to watch the boats traffic on the clear water. Some ducks swam by and he pulled pieces from the frankfurter roll, calling, "Here, duck. Here, duck, duck, duck," until he looked up and saw a small boy watching him very seriously. Max moved away and ate his lunch at the refreshment stand.

After lunch he started walking again. The park

stretched itself out before him, sun splashed lazy green hills and sentinel trees with fewer and fewer people the farther he went. He decided to walk all the way to the ocean.

A great fog met him at the beach, rolling in on its own tide, huge and slow and devouring everything in its way. Max could see the clear air behind him, over the Park, and then it was gone as the fog swept past, condensing on his glasses and causing him to shiver in its cold wet embrace. Stepping down to the beach, he walked out to where the water died at his feet He could count the number of times he had seen the Pacific, even after so many years in California. This was his fifth visit to the beach. Swimming was not allowed here because of the undertow and the ocean was too big to look at for very long without some part of him drowning. He reached down and accepted a gift of seaweed.

In Tel Aviv he had stood on the beach where his ancestors must have stood when they wanted relief from the desert. Watching the gray Pacific leap at the shore, he remembered Israel and his boundless history. Some eternal grandfather had skimmed stones into the Mediterranean and Max faced this strange ocean not even sure any more what tribe that ancestor belonged to. Well, Max, he told himself, this is as far as you can go.

Now his lungs wheezed with wet air and he wondered why he made himself come. The lights of the amusement park reached out through the fog. That's where the bus would be and he hurried, feeling his sinuses beginning to close.

As the bus shot along the misty street, Max leaned his forehead against the window to press away the pain that grew there. Nothing was clear in the fog, but at one stop, running for the bus as it pulled away from the curb, Max thought he saw the boy from the park, though he could not be sure. He opened the window and leaned out, but the figure vanished in the fog as the bus rolled down the street. Max could see his face more clearly when he closed his eyes. He remembered how he almost called the police to tell them about the boy and now that they found the one who did it, the Nazi, he was glad he hadn't. He had the idea that what happened was connected somehow to the years he spent in the concentration camp and he wondered if the boy might be Jewish. He closed his eyes: the blond hair, the short nose. He guessed not.

Max settled back in the seat, his stomach beginning to compete with his head for attention. He had not had anything to eat since the frankfurter at the lake and it was Sunday so he decided to treat himself to a big dinner at the Russian restaurant on Geary Boulevard, but as the bus pulled up to the stop it occurred to him that he did not have enough money with him. A quick check of his wallet showed him he was right; he would have to go home first.

His own street was only two stops farther, but when he stepped off the bus into the chilling grip of the fog and thought of the walk to his house and then the longer walk back to the restaurant he fingered the money in his pocket again, thinking there was enough for a hamburger; but he had promised himself a big dinner and with his lungs already choking and his head beginning to throb he made himself as small as he could and hurried home.

For a few minutes he stood in the middle of the room and forgot why he had come. Then his stomach announced itself and he remembered dinner and the money, but the little purse he kept in the drawer with his underwear contained only four dollars. It was the end of the month. He would need at least four dollars more for dinner and with the change he had he was still short almost fifty cents. An empty purse, he told himself, speaks louder than an empty stomach. He took two aspirins and considered doing without dinner; he could, he knew the small hunger that gnawed at his stomach was a joke. He remembered the time they had gone three days with nothing to eat and the fat Kommandant blamed it on the Allied planes, then on the fourth day they were given potato soup that was so thin one of the young people in the camp tore a notice off the wall and sunk it in his bowl and then went up and down the lines showing everyone that the notice could be read right through the soup until he was seized by a guard and beaten and later sentenced to solitary confinement for destroying an official notice. Max sighed, the slightly vocal gasp of air that expressed sorrow and disgust and weariness with being sorrowful and disgusted. The hunger was a bad joke, and the aspirin was not doing any good. He tried to think of where he might find fifty cents.

He tried his coat pocket and was rewarded by sixty cents in change and a button. He quickly put on his coat and prepared to go out to eat when he took a closer look at the button: it was not his. It was a strange button and even before he held it against the buttons on his coat he knew it was not his. This button was light blue and there was a pink flower engraved on it. It was clearly a girl's button. Max held it in his hand and wondered where he got it. He tried it again hopelessly against the buttons on his coat and then he set it down and stared at it as if it had come from another world. Max tried to remember when he had worn the coat last. It had been that night in the park and remembering that, Max tried to hold back what came next; the boy had thrown it away. Max remembered it hitting the tree and rolling back on the path. And what was the boy doing with a girl's button? And then Max did hold it back. He jammed the button back into the pocket it had come from and he hurried down the stairs and out into the foggy night. On his way to the restaurant he stopped and took the button out and threw it as far as he could across the wide street.

The few people left in the restaurant were finishing their dinners and the first two dishes Max ordered were all gone, so he ordered piroshkes which he knew would lie heavy on his stomach but it was the one treat left to him and then that was spoiled because he found himself staring at the buttons on the waitress' uniform and then at the buttons on the coats on the coatrack and when his soup came he thought for a minute he saw the pink and blue button floating in the soup. Then the piroshkes came and they were dry and tasteless as sand in his mouth.

"Anything wrong?" the waitress asked.

He shook his head, paid for the dinner, and left the restaurant, leaving most of the meal on the plate. He did not go straight home. On legs that had turned to jelly he crossed the street and began looking for the button. Among the trash at the gutter's edge he looked and along the fog shrouded sidewalk. "Damn thing," he cursed, stooping and poking at the old newspapers and candy wrappings. He tried going back to the other side of the street and standing where he stood when he threw it. Then, following the arc it must have followed, he crossed to the other side again and looked in doorways and tried scraping his foot along the sidewalk. People stopped and asked what he was looking for. Max waved them away, but some of them started looking anyway. "What are we looking for?" a man said on his knees, combing the sidewalk with his hand. "The Golden Gate Bridge," Max shouted, and while people laughed he found it finally alien and waiting, balanced on the edge of the sewer. One kick would send it away forever. He picked it up and with people beginning to crowd around to see what he had found he thrust it into his pocket and went home. Behind him, people continued to search the sidewalk.

5

Shmuel stood in front of Max's desk holding a three-page letter written in green ink. "It's from Mrs. Katz," he said.

Max pointed to his in basket and went on working.

"You don't feel well?" Shmuel observed.

"I feel fine."

His mouth was dry and his stomach empty and he could not remember having fallen asleep last night.

"You look terrible," Shmuel observed.

"Don't look so much," Max said, but later he wished he had someone to talk to and he was sorry he had sent Shmuel away. There had been nothing in the paper that morning about the case and again Max had the feeling that it was a dream, something that came and went like the fog. All morning he mechanically shuffled papers, then, on his way to lunch, he stopped at Shmuel's desk.

"I want to ask you something, Shmuel."

Shmuel waited, crouched behind his desk like a man in a trench. "*Nu?*"

"Nothing," Max said, and he hurried to the luncheonette. He had a grilled cheese sandwich and a milk shake, but the waitress with the big hands was not there.

It worried him that there was nothing in the papers about the case. All afternoon he tried to reconstruct the murder. In his mind the boy and the young Nazi took turns climbing on the girl until he yelled "Stop!" and the office

35

seemed to shudder and go very still.

Shmuel dropped the pile of outgoing mail when Max yelled The receptionist looked in she saw Shmuel picking up the mail and asked if anything was wrong. Shmuel shook his head and she left.

"What's the matter, Max?" Shmuel asked. He put the mail back on his desk and came to Max cautiously, as if he were approaching a barking dog.

"Nothing. I was thinking out loud."

Shmuel stood a minute. He shuffled his feet and asked, "Can I help, Max?"

"Go away," Max said. "Get out of here and leave me alone for once. You can't help. You stink. You know that Shmuel? Don't you ever take a bath?"

Shmuel stared. He smelled himself and shrugged his shoulders. "Max?"

It was five o'clock. Max got up and left, brushing past Shmuel and turning so that Shmuel could not see that he was weeping. Outside, he leaned against the building and bit his cheek. When he heard someone coming out, he ran to the corner, thinking, Tomorrow I'll apologize. He blamed his lack of sleep.

He bought a newspaper, praying there would be a story on the case, but though he scanned each page while waiting for the bus and examined each page again closely on the bus, he could not find anything about it. His hand trembled as he turned the last page; the paper made a noise that annoyed the man sitting next to him and Max tried to fold it quietly, but the last page was covered by a full-page advertisement for cigarettes, just as he remembered it was. Max saw that his hand was covered with newsprint. Although a cool breeze blew through the city, he was perspiring.

The bus was in the park before Max realized he had

passed his stop. He got off at the next stop and walked slowly and fearfully toward the place where the murder had occurred, watching the bushes as if he expected someone to jump out at him again. On his way he discovered the newspaper still in his hand and, cursing in German, he hurled it into the nearest trash basket. His hands were still trembling though he knew he would find nothing but a plot of grass.

The bushes were beaten down and candy wrappers and a beer can lay on the grass. Max walked around the little clearing, but there was nothing to see and he did not know what he was looking for anyway. He stayed until the first passerby noticed him, peering into the clearing and saying "Excuse me?" as if he had caught Max doing something obscene.

That evening he gave up his book to watch television with the Thompsons. He had set out to read all of Thomas Mann over again, in English this time, but he found it slow going and now, halfway through *The Magic Mountain*, he kept thinking how pleasant it would be to have tuberculosis. He imagined giving his body over to germs and doctors. Everything out of his hands. Finally he put the book away and went downstairs to watch the news on television.

"Been to the park lately?" Mrs. Thompson asked.

"The park?" Max shook his head.

There was a variety show on and Max was sorry he had come down so early. He wanted to go back upstairs and wait for the news, but the old man told him to have a seat and Max was trapped. He sat through the program, Mrs. Thompson knitting and her husband laughing and slapping his thigh at each joke, but none of them spoke. Then at eleven o'clock the news came on, but there was no mention of the case.

"Do you remember that murder in the park?" Max asked, but the opening credits for an old movie began and the old man put his finger to his pursed lips and turned up the volume while his wife went on knitting besides the china cat. Max said good night.

There was a story in the paper the next day that said Holtz appeared in court where he pled not guilty and was denied bail. Half-way to work Max got off the bus and took a taxi to the Hall of Justice.

The gray stone building stood huge and mausoleum-like in a graveyard of rotting homes and old warehouses; even the windows could not keep it from looking solid. Max hesitated. He expected to see prisoners handcuffed to policemen being dragged into the building, but there were only peaceful-looking people alone or in groups of two or three. Occasionally a woman with a small child walked briskly towards the building with no more fear or deliberation than if they were going shopping. Some looked up as they walked, inspecting the neat rows of windows as if to see what was on sale. With these people walked a few well dressed men with briefcases; they did not look up. Max fell in step behind a middle aged couple who were having difficulty keeping up with their lawyer already pushing his way through the bronze door.

The lobby was lined with brown marble and it too was not as Max had imagined. The people who came in the door with him broke in various directions and Max stood in the center of the large room and wondered why he had come. Then he remembered: he had come to see Holtz. It occurred to Max on his way to work that if he could just get a good look at Holtz he would know whether or not he was guilty. A man with a briefcase paused to light a cigarette and Max started to ask him for help, but the man moved on before Max could get his attention. In one corner of the room was a large information desk with several men ranged behind it, some busy answering questions. Max approached it and waited until a man in a crew cut and a square jaw stood opposite him and asked him what he wanted.

"I want to see Mr. Holtz please." But his request drowned in the noise of the lobby.

"What?"

"I want to see Mr. Holtz. Mr. Mortimer Holtz."

"Is he a prisoner?" the information officer asked.

"Yes. Of course he is a prisoner."

The officer took out a form. "Are you his father?"

"No," Max said. He looked about, hoping to find someone else to talk to. This man didn't seem to Max to know what he was doing. "No, I'm not his father."

"Are you his lawyer?"

"No. I just want to see him."

"Sorry," the officer said, returning the form to its drawer. "Only attorneys and immediate family are allowed to visit prisoners."

"I just want to see him for a minute," Max said.

The officer repeated the rule.

"But you don't understand. This is very important."

"I don't make the rules," the officer said, turning to someone else and leaving Max leaning against the counter with no one to talk to.

Max walked about the lobby. He found the men's room and he went in and urinated and then washed his hands and carefully combed his hair. There seemed to be fewer people in the lobby when he came out, but he was the only one who stood still. He felt a chill now, as if the coldness of the marble walls had reached him, and he began to walk to warm up. People headed for elevators and Max wondered why he couldn't just go up and see

Holtz. Imagining a row of cells with prisoners pacing back and forth in each one, he thought if he could just find the right cell he could see Holtz before anyone else asked him if he was Holtz's father. There was a news and candy stand near him and he asked the operator where the prisoners were kept.

"Take the elevator here to the sixth floor."

Max turned around and saw the elevator. "Thank you," he said, and went to press the button. See, he told himself, it's easy.

When the elevator doors opened on the sixth floor he found himself confronted by bars. He had just room enough to take two steps off the elevator which closed behind him. With the bars in front and the closed door of the elevator behind him, Max suddenly felt he had made a terrible mistake. The chill came back and he put his shaking hands in his pockets. A policeman came up on the other side of the bars.

"Who do you want to see?"

Max stared at him, unable to decide whether to speak or turn and press the elevator button and hope the elevator came before anything further happened. Behind the officer Max could see two rows of small, glass enclosed rooms. In several of them people sat and talked. Perhaps the officer downstairs was wrong, he thought.

"Who do you want to see?" the policeman repeated.

Or perhaps having come this far, he would be allowed to see Holtz without being asked any more questions. He made up his mind and said, "I would like to see Mr. Mortimer Holtz."

"Let's see your pass."

Max's heart sank. He took his hands out of his pockets and took hold of the bars to steady himself. "I don't have a pass."

The policeman told him he would have to get a pass at the information desk in the lobby.

"Even if I just want to see him for a minute? You don't even have to take him out of the cell," Max said, already backing away from the bars.

"Sorry. No visiting without a pass."

Max turned and rang for the elevator. Then he turned again and called the policeman back. "Excuse me," he said. "Can anyone get a pass?"

"Immediate family and attorneys only."

Max thanked him and stepped into the elevator. He wondered what would happen if he told the man downstairs that he was Holtz's attorney.

In the lobby again he waited until the officer he first spoke to was busy. Then he went up to another man at the information desk and asked for a pass to see Mortimer Holtz.

"Relation?"

"I'm his attorney," Max said.

"Can I see your credentials?"

"Credentials?" Max started to reach for his wallet. The information officer waited. "I left them at home," Max said. "I'll come back." He retreated across the lobby; when he got to the door he looked back to see if anyone was following him. No one was and Max stopped and felt a fist of rage in his stomach. It was too late to go to work now and he didn't know what to do with himself for the rest of the day. He stopped at the newsstand to buy a paper.

"Have you seen Holtz, the murderer?" he asked the newsstand operator.

"No," the man said, chuckling as he reached for Max's quarter.

Then Max looked up and saw that the man was blind. He ran out of the building and vomited in the gutter.

6

All night he wrestled with a chill that ravaged his body. Wearing a sweater over his pajamas and lying under every blanket he could find with his coat thrown on top, he wavered between sleep and waking. Once he put his icy fingers to his cheeks and swore he would not make such a fool of himself again as he had at the Hall of Justice. Just before dawn, he threw up. After cleaning up the mess, he stopped at the window and saw the dark sky open just over the roofs of the houses. He took a deep breath and then went back to bed and immediately fell asleep.

When the alarm rang in the morning he sat up and discovered that he was not even tired. His cheeks were warm again and warmth flowed down to his fingers and toes. He thought about breakfast and it occurred to him that he might be out of eggs, but he soon discovered that there were two left and much relieved he put the water on for coffee and went to wash. While he shaved he thought about growing a beard; he trimmed the stubble on his cheeks and over his lip and then he washed away the rest of the lather and studied the effect in the mirror. There was not enough beard to tell but he decided after turning his head from side to side that his face was too small to support a beard. He lathered up again and finished shaving. It was not until after breakfast as he sat back and chewed the last of his third slice of toast that he thought of Holtz and the boy. He wondered what they must have thought of him at the Hall of Justice, a crazy old man trying to see a prisoner he didn't even know. Well, he had tried, and he was lucky he hadn't gotten himself arrested. As he dressed he thought about it once more, but it was already beginning to fade from his mind, ebbing away like a tide. How close he had come to getting involved. After all, he thought, *Das geht mich nichst an.* And remembering the resolution he made when he first came to the United States, he said it out loud in English: "It's none of my business." He had sworn never to speak German again.

At work he had to explain to everyone that he had not come in yesterday because of an upset stomach. Only Shmuel was not satisfied.

"A kind of burning sensation up here?" he asked, jumping up and indicating the area just under his ribs.

"Not exactly," Max said.

"Have you had out your appendicitis?"

"Yes," Max said. "I had my appendix out a long time ago."

Dr. Resnick came in to tell Max that he borrowed some folders while Max was out. He put the folders on Max's desk. When he left, Shmuel came over.

"You know the best thing to settle a stomach?"

"Leave me alone, Shmuel. I have lots of work." Max indicated the pile of letters and folders on his desk.

"You make some strong tea and you put in it honey and lemon and a little *shnapps.* That's what my mother always made if she was sure it wasn't the appendicitis."

Max looked across the desk at Shmuel who stood stooped and not much higher standing than Max was sitting. Under Max's scrutiny Shmuel first smiled and then frowned, wrinkling his forehead like a piece of parchment. Max leaned out over his desk and pointed his finger. "Why don't you go back to Poland, Shmuel, with your quack cures?"

Shmuel retreated half way across the room. "Don't talk like that, Max. You know I've thought about going back. There's no one there for me any more."

Max suddenly saw his finger pointing at Shmuel's desk as if at Poland. He withdrew it and said, "I didn't mean it literally."

Shmuel turned and walked bent over to his desk. When he sat down he faced the door so that Max had only his back to look at. Something seemed to grow in Max's throat; he swallowed hard and said, "I'm sorry, Shmuel. I didn't mean anything. Open the mail already."

For once there was enough work to keep Max busy all day. It was really a part time job and if he could afford it he would suggest that he come in every other day, or else work only in the mornings. The only other solution he could think of was to fire Shmuel and take over both jobs himself. He thought about this, but then he shrugged his shoulders and reminded himself that hiring and firing was Dr. Resnick's job not his and he put a pile of folders in the out basket and told Shmuel they were ready.

The rest of the week went by quickly. On Friday there was a letter from Mrs. Greenberg in Mexico. Her husband was having second thoughts about the baby she was carrying; he threatened to go back to San Francisco and kill the father. Max pulled her folder out of the dead file, resisted the temptation to write *I told you so!* on it, added the letter to the folder and with a sigh tossed the whole thing into the box to go to Dr. Resnick again.

He seldom thought about Holtz and the boy: Sometimes, when he thought he was thinking about something else, he would find them lurking in the corners of his mind, but when he found them there he dismissed them as he might dismiss the memory of an old movie or a dimly remembered drama and his life became as smooth as a tide washed beach.The whole affair in the park seemed to be slipping from the public memory as well, though he could not be sure of this for he stopped buying newspapers and he seldom heard the news on the radio, but no one talked about it any more and even Mrs. Thompson stopped asking him if he still went to the park at night. By Friday he was more interested in the Goldman case than in the park murder. Mr. Goldman's teenage wife had disappeared while they were vacationing in New Orleans. Goldman said she had been kidnapped, but the New Orleans police were inclined to believe she had deserted him. Now Goldman, back in San Francisco, was appealing to the agency for help. Of course she deserted, Max thought, suspecting that Goldman was very rich and had bribed the girl to marry him. What did he expect? And with that, Max began to think about his own vacation which was only a week away.

Every year Max went to visit his cousin Morris in Los Angeles. Morris had helped bring Max to America. When Morris came to San Francisco they had dinner together and each summer Max spent his vacation with Morris and his family. At first Morris only wanted to talk about Germany and what it had been like in the camps. He gave Max books that described the Nazi atrocities. "Tell me if this book is true," he would say. "Was it really like that?" Max would read the first page or two and the next morning at breakfast he would say, "Yes, that's the way it was." But Morris finally ran out of books, or else his wife convinced him that Max did not like to talk about it, so now they did not talk about anything at all. Georgia went to all the movie screenings and she would tell Max the plots in great detail, but she always spoke to Max very slowly and distinctly and a little louder than she spoke to anyone else. It was the way, Max noticed, she spoke to the Japanese clerk at the cleaners. The boy, Arthur, was fifteen now and they did not exchange anything but hello and goodbye.

Once he was there, Max counted the days until it was time to go back to San Francisco.

He thumbed through the folders on his desk and wondered if Morris would be insulted if this year he went somewhere else. On his way home he stopped to look at the posters in the travel agency windows on Geary Boulevard. There was a picture of a beach in Hawaii with a young couple running toward an indigo ocean. He closed his eyes and imagined himself lying in the warm sand. The trouble with a vacation like that, he told himself, is that it left you with nothing to do but wonder who you were and what you were doing there. In the next window, a poster advertised a tour of England called "Shakespeare's Country." He went inside and got a folder describing the tour. Back in his room he tried to imagine himself touring Stratford. "To go or not to go?" he asked himself in the mirror. Finally, he decided that he could not face going back to Europe, not even to England, so he sat down and wrote to Morris, telling him when he would arrive.

The night before his vacation began he told the Thompsons he would be gone for two weeks. They were just finishing dinner and Mr. Thompson said, "Have a good time," and went into the living room to turn on the television. Mrs. Thompson was still cleaning up. "Are you going to Los Angeles again this year?" she asked.

"Yes. To see my cousin."

Mrs. Thompson finished clearing the table and began stacking the dishes in the dishwasher. Max did not know whether to leave or offer to help. Over the noise of the machine she said, "That's where I would like to live, but Fred says he can't stand the smog."

Max murmured agreement and started to back out of the kitchen, but Mrs. Thompson patted back her hair and began to speak before he got out of the room.

46

"I used to go there often before my sister passed away. Once I almost met Clark Gable." She sat down and her eyes sparkled with memory. "It was at a party and he was supposed to be there. I stayed until three in the morning, but he never came. Of course, I was younger then."

"That's too bad," Max said.

"Well," she said. "I know you'll have a good time there."

Max went upstairs to pack.

7

Georgia met him at the station, explaining that Morris was working late. Morris was a salesman for a company that manufactured hospital equipment and the thing Max liked best about his house was that all the beds except Arthur's were hospital beds and Max could raise the top half of his bed when he wanted to read or the lower half when he wanted to rest his legs. Once he raised both halves and Morris had to come and get him out because he developed a cramp. "He's meeting with one of the directors of a new sanitarium that's opening in Pasadena," Georgia said. "It could mean a big sale."

"Well, lots of luck to him."

Georgia had dyed her hair again; it was black this time and curiously thick, as if she had dyed it with shoe polish. Max would have complimented her on it just so she would know he noticed, but they were on the freeway and he was busy keeping an eye on the flying traffic around them. When they got to the house he said, "Your hair looks very nice."

"Do you think so?" she asked. "I don't like it too

much, but it is very nice of you to say you like it."

They had the same conversation every year. Max wished she would leave her hair alone, brunette with splinters of gray. She did one year and Max told her it looked very distinguished, but she dyed it the next day.

Georgia called Arthur down from his room to say hello and then she excused herself to make dinner. As soon as she was gone, Arthur went back to his room. Max looked about. The only new thing was a picture over the electric fireplace where a mirror used to be. It was a full-size reproduction of a Van Gogh wheatfield; the brush strokes were so real that Max looked twice and then got up to examine it, even touching it before he sat down with the feel of the deceptive cardboard still in his fingers. The rest of the living room was the same: comfortable modern furniture, a champagne colored wall-to-wall carpet (when they first got it, Max remembered, Georgia made everyone take their shoes off when entering the living room), shelves with an assortment of books and glass knick knacks, and a television radio phonograph combination, but Morris would want Max to notice the picture so he made a mental note to mention it. Through the picture window Max could see the man in the house across the way standing by his window. The man saw Max and turned away. Max picked up an ash tray from the coffee table; it was of blue stone and had been made in Israel. Max held it awhile and then he put it down and went to his room and unpacked.

"I was looking all over for you," Georgia said as he put the last of his socks away, "but I see you found your room all by yourself." She announced dinner and Max washed and joined Georgia and Arthur in the kitchen.

"I hope you don't mind if we eat in the kitchen tonight," she apologized, serving him a slice of meat loaf.

Max waved his hand. Georgia sat down and then suddenly, as if she just remembered to say grace, looked from Max to Arthur and asked, "Well, did you two have a nice conversation while I was busy?"

Arthur looked down at his plate. Max said they had, and as always when he told a lie, he entered into the book of his life a mark on the debit side. He began to eat. The meat loaf was very good and he said so. "That's very sweet," Georgia said. Then he asked Arthur how he was doing in school and the only other thing that came to his mind was the picture and he was saving that for Morris. As if reading his mind, Georgia said, "Morris will be home around nine o'clock."

After dinner Arthur excused himself and left the house. Georgia cleared the table while Max made himself comfortable in the living room. He was almost asleep when Georgia came in.

"How's your job, Max?" she asked, lighting a cigarette.

"It's all right."

"You have a lot of responsibility, don't you? I mean, the fate of all those people is practically in your hands."

Over the years Max had exaggerated his job, adding duties as Morris and Georgia demanded to know how he was getting on. "Responsibility is a good thing," he said. "It makes a person feel useful."

"I saw a television program about a social worker the other night." She told him all about the program. When he interrupted to tell her he was not a social worker she said, "No, but this man in the television program was, you see."

"That sounds like a good program," Max said when she was finished.

After a while, Georgia began to hum. She had once taken voice lessons. Her voice was not bad and she told

Max that she was going to be another Jeanette MacDonald. Max did not know who Jeanette MacDonald was. "That's very nice," he said. He stretched all the muscles in his body he could to stay awake, the way a cat does when she uncoils from sleep.

A little after nine the door chimes rang. "That's Morris," Georgia said, hurrying to the door. Max stood up and straightened his suit.

Morris stepped into the house and kissed Georgia on the cheek. "Have you had a good day, dear?" he asked, putting his briefcase down and picking up the evening paper.

"Come on, you phony," Georgia said. "Did you do it?"

Morris examined the newspaper until a smile broke his face. He nodded, throwing the paper away and embracing Georgia. "They'll have to confirm it tomorrow, but it's a sure thing. Fifty beds, Georgia, and all the nightstands and bedpans that go with it."

"My hero!" Georgia kissed him, then pushed him off, saying, "Your cousin Max is here."

Morris came to Max and they shook hands. "Hello, Max. You look wonderful." They stepped back to examine each other.

Morris was beginning to surrender to overweight; all the angles of his face had softened and his stomach bulged pregnantly. His thick, wavy hair was still black on top but feathered out to a soft white around the fringe and thick glasses gave his eyes a startled look. He had gone to Hollywood as an actor in 1939 and it was in that same year that Max was told by his mother that he had a cousin named Morris Glick in Los Angeles, U.S.A. Max remembered that all through the war.

"Congratulations, Morris," Max said, shaking his hand again. "You must be some salesman."

"Thank you, Max."

Georgia said she would make some coffee. "Then you have to tell us just how you made the sale."

"Listen, honey, we really ought to celebrate. How about a big party Friday night?"

"Wonderful," Georgia said, but her face darkened and after she went into the kitchen she called Morris in to help her. Max heard their voices getting louder. He thought they would want to be alone to talk about the big sale and he was unable to stretch away his tiredness so he started for the kitchen to tell Georgia he didn't want any coffee, but he heard his name and he stood outside the door and listened. "What about Max?" Morris was asking.

"Won't he be out of place?"

"He'll be all right. If it gets too late for him he'll just go to sleep."

"Go to sleep? How will he be able to sleep with a party going on?"

"Listen," Morris whispered, "he slept through a war, didn't he?"

Max hurried back to the living room. When Georgia and Morris came in with the coffee, Max mentioned the picture.

"Do you like it?" Morris asked. He passed a little tray with sugar and cream on it to Max. "We used to have a mirror there but someone got drunk at a party one night and broke it. Threw her shoe right at it. I think she saw herself in the mirror and thought someone was wearing the same dress she was wearing." Morris and Georgia both laughed. Max, pouring cream into his coffee, imagined the scene and smiled. "We picked it out ourselves," Morris said, and Georgia added, "It matches the rug." Then Morris began to tell about the sale.

Max spent most of the week trying to stay out of

51

everyone's way. Once he went to the beach. He did not go swimming, but he lay on the beach in a borrowed bathing suit and watched the young men showing off their muscles and the children building castles of wet sand. One little girl was naked and Max thought of Mann's "Mario and the Magician" and the commotion caused by the naked little girl on the beach in Italy. No one here was upset. When he looked around he saw several more children with nothing on, and the women hardly wore more. Max did not approve of nudity, but he did not complain. We can stand to be more like children, he thought. And he remembered that it was the adults who chased the little girl in Mann's story who were soon making war. He wanted to talk about this to Morris or Georgia, but the moment never seemed right and on Friday, while Georgia cleaned the house and set out glasses and whiskey bottles on the portable bar, Max took a nap, determined to stay awake as long as the party lasted.

The guests began arriving at eight o'clock and by ten the living room was forested with people. Max met a baby photographer and his wife, several salesmen from the company Morris worked for, a high school teacher and her husband, and a man who played bit parts in movies before Morris and Georgia gave up introducing him to people as they came in. Max stayed near the door for a while, nodding to unfamiliar faces and waiting for someone to speak to him. Once he answered the door when no one else seemed to hear the chimes and a tall thin man with white hair and a deep voice said, "Good evening," and handed Max his coat.

No one else came. Max wandered through the living room, stopping by different clusters of people to listen in on the conversation and see if anyone would talk to him. The baby photographer said, "Hey, you're not drinking anything," so Max went into the kitchen and got a glass of water which he took back into the living room to drink, using the empty glass to make himself less conspicuous, but when he passed the bar a fat man Max did not remember meeting took the glass from him and replaced it with a scotch and soda. Max carried it around for the next hour, nodding to people and holding his highball up. For a while he got into a conversation with a man who had just moved to Los Angeles from the Bay Area. "San Francisco is very pretty when you can see it," the man said, "but who can live in all that fog? Down here the sun comes out and brings me to life. Heat, that's what man needs. More heat."

Max wanted to say something about the smog, but Morris put the phonograph on very loud and Max just nodded. A tall woman balancing a martini in one hand was arguing with Georgia. The tall woman wanted to roll the rug back so they could dance, but Georgia finally got her to agree to dance on the patio and several couples headed that way. "I better keep an eye on my wife," the man who had recently moved to Los Angeles said, and he left Max and caught up with the tall woman at the door to the patio. Max stationed himself by the canapé tray and nibbled crackers spread with chopped liver. He sipped at his drink and watched the crowd pair off to dance. Someone hit his arm in passing and some of the whiskey sloshed out of the glass and onto his pant leg. He was wiping it off with his handkerchief when a large woman with bleached blond hair appeared and helped him, wiping the whiskey with her own little handkerchief. "There!" she said, as if her handkerchief had succeeded where his had failed.

"Thank you," Max said.

She bulged in her dress in odd places as if she had been shoveled into it. "Would you care to dance?" she asked.

"No, thank you," Max said, flattered that she would ask.

"You're not being bashful now, are you?" she said.

"I really don't know how to dance. Tell you the truth, I don't like it." He saw her looking around and afraid she was searching for another partner he added quickly, "It's very nice out there on the patio, though."

"I was just looking for the bar. Would you get me a martini?"

Max found the bar again and stared at the bottles. He looked about for Morris but found the fat man instead. "Fill her up?" the man said, pouring some more scotch into Max's glass. Max asked him if he could make a martini. "Well, it's better not to mix your drinks," the fat man said.

"It's not for me."

The fat man winked and made the martini and then Max took it back and found the blond sitting on the couch.

"Thank you." She sipped the drink. "My name is Verna Finchley. You're Morris's cousin, aren't you?"

"Yes. Max Friedman."

They talked about Los Angeles. Then she said, "I understand you were in a concentration camp, you poor man."

Max silently cursed his cousin. "Yes," he said.

"Well, you needn't worry about me. I'm not going to ask you for the gory details." She laughed, and then, laying her hand on his shoulder, "I know you don't want to be reminded of it."

"Thank you, madam."

She took another sip of her martini and Max drank a bit from his scotch and soda.

"Besides," she said suddenly, her voice cheerful again, "I've seen plenty of it in the movies and Lord knows they don't spare you any of the details, do they? Did you see *Judgement At Nuremberg* on TV?"

"No." He almost saw it. The Thompsons called him down. He watched until the first break and then he said he wasn't feeling well and excused himself. He heard Mr. Thompson say, "I hope they show the atrocities."

Verna Finchley finished her drink and said, "It's all about this American army captain who goes to Nuremberg to be a judge at the trial of some Nazi war criminals."

"Yes," Max said, getting up.

"He meets Marlene Dietrich," she said, but Max interrupted. "Excuse me," he said, "but I just saw someone I have to speak to," and without looking back he went out on the patio to laugh at himself and at Verna Finchley and at his cousins Morris and Georgia. The night air was good, but he entered another mark on the debit side.

A few couples danced to the music that drifted out from the phonograph and the conversation and laughter in the living room came with it, like bubbles at Max's back. Someone came running out on the patio chasing an ice cube and the dancers jumped about and whooped and giggled until he caught it and dropped it in his drink to the cheers of people inside and out. "The Dodgers could use you," the baby photographer yelled in a surprising bullhorn voice. Max moved away from the laughter and leaned against the wall where it was dark. He spilled the rest of his drink into a bush and then he tried to locate through the clouds and haze of city lights the north star and the next thing he knew he was in a chair at the edge of the patio just rising from sleep. The party was still going on, though only one couple danced now. By his watch it was one o'clock, but he didn't know how long he had slept. It was the drink, he decided, and he looked around for the glass he knew he had been holding. It was not by the chair; he looked by the door and by the wall where he had been standing, but he could not find it so he shrugged his shoulders and, hoping no one had stepped on it, he went inside to see if he could go to his room without Morris or Georgia seeing him.

There was an argument going on in the living room. A man Max had been introduced to earlier, a dentist named La Vine, was backed against the wall by a young man who kept poking him in the chest as he spoke.

"It's none of your damn business," the dentist said.

"He's drunk," a man said, reaching out of the surrounding crowd to pull the young man away. He could not get a grip on the young man's shoulder and no one helped him.

Max asked the woman next to him what was happening. She told him that La Vine had been a witness to a recent incident in which a man was beaten up on a downtown street. Along with other onlookers, he had done nothing to stop it. The young man recognized him from a picture in the paper and started the argument.

"Why should I get involved?" the dentist said, appealing to the crowd.

Max started to go to his room, but he saw Morris and Georgia conferring by the hallway and he decided to stay and listen.

"Where's your pride?" the young man shouted, "your sense of responsibility? You live in a world with other people, not by yourself." He indicated the people around him.

"If you were there you would understand," the dentist said. "I didn't know either of the men. It wasn't any of my business and it's none of yours either."

"I ask you," the young man said, turning to the crowd, "would you want this man for a neighbor?"

Some people laughed; the baby photographer cried, "Why not?" and someone said, "You're drunk," and tried to reach for him again. Max saw Morris and Georgia coming over and he slipped away on the other side of the crowd and went to his room.

The argument was over but the party continued and the noise drifted into Max's room. The phonograph started again and the music seemed to carry the noise away, but as Max slept it carried back again and in his dreams Max heard *Das geht mich nichts an. Das geht mich nichts an.*

When he awoke, Max listened to the stillness of the house. He dressed quietly and went to look at the living room. Everyone had disappeared, leaving behind glasses and bottles and brimming ashtrays. Where the two men had argued only an empty bottle stood on the floor. Going by Morris and Georgia's bedroom, Max heard Morris snoring. He went hack to his own room, got his coat, and went out for a walk.

The boy and the Nazi and the murdered girl had all crept back into his mind while he slept. He walked faster as if to escape them and soon he found himself in an unfamiliar neighborhood. The gable roofed houses where his cousin lived, each on a separate carpet of grass, had yielded to smaller houses; the grass became strips between them, and now the grass was gone and apartment houses lined the street with only an apron of pavement before them. Max looked at his watch, but it had stopped. It could not be too early: women with shopping carts were out and children were playing in the street. On the next block Max stopped, astonished to see a synagogue. He stared at the familiar six-pointed star and the tablets with the Hebrew inscription. The doors were open, some people were still going in. Max had not been to synagogue since he came to America: Cautiously he crossed the street to read the bulletin hoard posted by the doors. A shammis, coming to close the doors, hesitated. Max turned to go. He heard the doors close and then, struck by a longing for exactly the same feeling that had kept him away all these years, the past, his past, that he knew was lurking behind doors like these,he turned again, bounded up the stairs, and slipped inside.

"*Gut Shabbos*," the shammis greeted him. Max nodded. Quickly he picked a paper yarmulke out of the box and seated himself on a rear bench.

He did not remember the prayers very well, but he could still read Hebrew and he stumbled along half a line or so behind the congregation. When he was bar mitzvahed he read a speech he had composed himself. He could still recall parts of it. Something about the law being a thing that lived in books while justice lived in the heart. Or perhaps his father had helped him with it; he couldn't remember. He seldom went to synagogue after that: when his mother died, when his nephew was bar mitzvahed, once or twice on the high holidays until his religion wore out like an old coat. His memory of Saturday mornings before he was thirteen was largely a memory of his grandfather and though they went together to the synagogue it was not the synagogue he remembered at all but Grandfather Mordecai in his caftan and broad brimmed hat. *We're among civilized people now*, the family would say to him. *Why don't you take off that outfit already?* And Grandfather Mordecai, catching at his beard and sucking in his breath in mock surprise, but still managing to wink at Max, would say, *You mean you want me to walk around naked?*

Grandfather Mordecai smelled of sweet wine and rich egg bread. He owned a tailor shop in which he worked long after he was too old for such work. Sometimes after supper Max went down to work in the shop to let Mordecai rest. It was only a matter of taking in the garments the customers brought and giving them the ones that were mended. Mordecai could sew at home. Max was supposed to be at the shop the night Mordecai was killed, but he said he had too much homework to do. They found Mordecai lying dead in the shop, his thick beard caked with blood and purple bruises covering his face, and on the window of the shop a Star of David crudely drawn with soap. "Thank God it wasn't the boy," Max heard his father say.

Max looked up. Around him the old men rocked in time to their prayers. In their silken shawls they looked as if they could be one of the ten tribes crossing the desert into oblivion and he remembered that Mordecai told him the Indians in America were definitely the lost tribes, though he could not decide now whether Mordecai had been serious or not. This synagogue was like the one he had known in Berlin until his father switched to the reform temple. Painted on the windows were the decalogue and the insignia of the twelve tribes and overhead was the balcony where the women sat. The synagogue in Berlin was bigger, but even now Max could almost hear outside, above the singing of the cantor, the marching boots of the SS.

He was several pages behind in the prayers. By the time he found the place the Torah was being carried around the room. Max edged his way to the end of the row where he could reach it as it went by. He touched it and then kissed his fingers as the others did, some with the tassels on their prayer shawls. That's right, he remembered, we don't kiss the book, it kisses us. Later, when it was time to remember the dead, he said a special prayer for Mordecai.

The service over, Max stumbled down the steps with his eyes squinted shut against the bright sun, as if he would open them on a revelation, but there was just a street full of people wishing each other a good day and beginning to talk about the weather and politics and baseball. He started to look for a bus, but then he decided to walk because it was such a nice day and it was, after all, the Sabbath.

On the way back to his cousin's house he came upon some children playing in the street. A boy in a blue polo shirt torn halfway down the back kneeled at a hydrant, counting "One, two, three, four..." while other boys scattered the length of the block to hide behind cars, in driveways, and behind garbage cans. Max stopped to watch. "...forty-nine, fifty. Anyone around my base is it," the boy concluded. Max could see a freckled face peer out around the corner of a house, a mop of blond hair rise cautiously over the hood of a car. The boy with the torn shirt walked slowly down the street. Another boy crept up to Max. "Let me walk next to you, Mister," the boy whispered. With the boy at his side, Max moved through the game, awkward and humble. Suddenly, the boy with the torn shirt saw the boy at Max's side and the two boys raced for the base. Max felt his heart lift. At the next corner he stopped to pat on the head a boy hiding behind a car and then he went on. Almost unaware of what he was thinking, he said to himself: *Yes, the boy is guilty. Holtz is innocent.* He reached the house and told Morris he had been for a walk.

That night he understood. He closed his eyes to sleep, but he opened them again and stared at the white ceiling as if the words were written there. He must not let Holtz die. He could not let Holtz suffer for something the boy did. He could not let Holtz become a kind of Jew.

8

In the morning his first thought was to go back to San Francisco immediately but he didn't know what to tell Morris. At breakfast Georgia asked him what was wrong.

"Nothing," Max said. "I was just thinking." If he said he was sick they would insist that he stay in Los Angeles, and he certainly couldn't tell them he had to go back to turn a boy over to the police. Then something occurred to him and he excused himself from the breakfast table and went into the living room to think about it. Suppose he went to the police and they wanted to know why he didn't tell them about the boy before? Suppose, he said to himself, they wanted to know what I was doing in the park that night? He began to pace back and forth. And what, he thought, if they can't find the boy, then what? He went back to the kitchen and sipped at his coffee.

"You're sure you're all right?" Morris asked.

"Sure," Max said. "I'm all right."

The next day Morris got him in to see a television show being taped and that night they watched the program, trying to see Max in the audience. "You should have waved your arm," Morris said. One day he went to the beach and another he did some shopping with Georgia. She had trouble finding pants to go with the blouse she bought the previous week and following her around from store to store, standing uncomfortably in the women's wear sections as she tried on and rejected what seemed to him like dozens of pairs of pants, it came to him like something tossed up by the tide: he would have to find the boy himself. Once the idea came to him, it seemed easy.

He would put the matter to him, appeal to his conscience, and when the boy understood that an innocent man was going to die in his place, then surely the boy would turn himself in. He even saw himself lecturing the boy on responsibility, going down to the police station with him so the boy would not be afraid, and the boy shaking his hand and thanking him as he was led away.

Max paced off the remaining days of the week as if he were himself imprisoned, sentenced to this vacation that prevented him from doing something important. When at last he was on the train, he sat on the edge of the seat, urging it forward. It was not until Sunday night when he stepped onto the platform in San Francisco that he asked himself how he was going to find the boy. People entering the station parted and went around him. The crowds disappeared into the lobby, and Max was alone on the sidewalk, asking himself over and over: *How in this entire city will I find him?* He took a taxi home.

At work the next morning he told everyone that he had a fine time. Only Shmuel wanted to hear all the details. "Leave me alone," Max told him. "I've got lots of work to do." Letters and folders were piled high on his desk and Max contemplated them with satisfaction. The work would help him get through the day quickly and after supper he would begin the search. He decided the boy must live in the vicinity of the park and he would walk the streets around there until he found him. There had not been time to shop so he had dinner in a cafeteria on Geary Boulevard and then, rehearsing to himself what he would say when he found him, started walking down one block and up another, looking for the blond boy with the cupid mouth and the pimples.

By the third night of his search he was out near the ocean, close enough anyhow to smell the salt and have the fog engulf him, pressing its cold wet hands against his face and cutting off his air like some maniac. He was discouraged. He might pass the boy right by and not recognize him. The boy might not live around here. He might have run away, gone to Mexico, India. Max took the bus home.

The next day the lining of his throat had gone raw. At work he sneezed in fits; he knew he was getting a cold and he cursed the boy and Holtz and the night he had gone to the park.

"You look like you need another vacation," Shmuel observed.

"Mind your own business, Shmuel," Max said as loudly as he could with his throat on fire.

Shmuel threw both his hands in the air. "I didn't say a word."

As soon as he felt better, he decided, he would go to the police, but it was Sunday before his head cleared and he was not sure the police would be open on the weekend. Monday afternoon he worked late replacing worn-out folders. He was the last one to leave. Standing on the corner, urging himself on to the police station, he suddenly heard another voice whispering: *The criminal always returns to the scene of the crime*, and with a quick surge of joy he boarded the bus for home, eager for night to come so he could try the little grove where the murder had taken place.

While he prepared dinner he relived that night. He could still feel traces of the terror that froze his heart when the boy leaped from the bushes. After he ate he paced the room, waiting for the sun to give up the day. It was just one month since the crime occurred; he was sure he would find the boy in the park.

Clutching the front of his coat with one hand and

reaching out to feel the black leaves along the path with the other, Max passed the bench he had sat on that night, stood by the grove, and came back to the bench to rest. *A man's life is in your hands,* he would say. *You cannot run from responsibility. Look at Eichmann!* That didn't sound right; he would not mention Eichmann. *A man's life is in your hands.* An hour passed. *We are all weighed on the scales of justice.* Another hour passed. What am I doing here like a *mishuganah?* he asked himself, and went home.

For two more days he searched the park, walking the paths near the grove or sitting on the bench where he sat that night pretending to read but examining the people who passed by. Once he even forced himself to go into the grove and stare at the spot where the girl had lain. He remembered the newspaper pictures but there was nothing there now, not even an indentation in the grass.

The next day he had a different idea; he would explore the neighborhood where the girl lived. Remembering that the newspaper had printed her address, he went through the old papers stacked in the Thompson's garage until he found it. She lived seven or eight blocks away on the other side of Geary and with that part of the paper torn out and thrust in his pocket he went to work and returned that afternoon not to his own house but to hers.

It was a street of cream colored stucco houses in the last neighborhood before the fancy homes with views of the Golden Gate or the Presidio. The girl's own house was in the middle of the street. The curtains were open but there was no sign of life. Max felt a terrific curiosity to look into her house. Cautiously he climbed the three steps to the door and listened for footsteps, prepared to run if anyone came. There was no sound so he leaned over as far as he could to look in the window. He could see a comfortable looking couch and a coffee table with newspapers on it. The floor was covered by an orange carpet and against the far wall on the mantle over the fireplace was a picture draped with a black cloth. He could not see the picture clearly but he knew it must be the girl.

"What do you want?" a voice in the street called.

Panicked, Max turned and saw a tall man with a round face and a pencil-thin moustache approaching.

"Does Shmuel Pinsky live here?" Max asked, his voice breaking.

"Get out of here!" the man said.

Max ran down the steps and mumbled an apology as he passed the man who went into the house. *Oy*, Max thought, the girl's father.

He hurried down the street. Two blocks away he saw a high school and he went there. Some boys were playing basketball in the yard but none of them looked like the boy he was looking for. On another street he came upon a luncheonette and when he went in he saw the boy in a booth. Max's heart stopped. For a moment he and the boy stared at each other as they had in the park, but the boy did not recognize him and resumed talking to his friends.

Max sat down at the counter and ordered a cup of coffee. He peeked over the menu at the boy. "Anything else?" the waitress asked.

As Max sipped his coffee the boy's friends left and Max wondered if he should join the boy in the booth. He rehearsed again what he would say. The boy got up, put some money down by the cash register, and left the luncheonette. Max quickly took another sip of the hot coffee, dropped fifty cents on the counter and followed the boy out.

Within half a block the boy sensed that he was being followed. He glanced back, but kept walking.

"Wait," Max shouted, hurrying to catch up. "I want to talk to you."

The boy looked back again but he did not stop.

Perspiring now, Max began to run. The boy disappeared around the corner. Max felt the muscles in his legs ache with an effort they had not made in many years. When he got to the corner he could not see the boy anywhere. He had to rest. Mopping his forehead, he thought, *Well, I've done my best.*

The boy stepped out of a doorway. "What do you want?" he asked.

Max dragged air into his lungs, trying to catch his breath. He studied the boy's face. There was a big pimple on the side of his nose and smaller pustules on his forehead which he had not noticed in the dim light of the park, but there was no doubt. This was the same boy. He even saw the same anxious look appear on his face.

"What do you want?" the boy repeated, taking a step backwards.

"I want to talk to you. A man's life is in your hands."

The boy backed away some more. "I don't know what you're talking about," he said, turning and walking away.

"I'll go to the police!" Max yelled.

The boy stopped. "What do you want from me?"

"I want you to give yourself up."

"For what? I didn't do anything." His voice cracked.

"Let's talk." Max looked around for a convenient place. All he could see besides houses was the edge of the Presidio, the big army reservation two blocks away. "Maybe over there," Max said, taking the boy's arm.

"Who are you?"

As they walked Max told the boy his name and what he had seen that night and told him about the button. The boy nodded. He remembered almost bumping into someone.

"What's your name?" Max asked.

"Harold. Harold Kirby."

So now the face that had haunted Max for so long had a name. He repeated it to himself. They walked the next block in silence, but when they came to the Presidio they saw there was a fence around it. On the road leading in there was a guard house. A soldier in a white helmet came out and looked at them so they continued walking.

"Why did you do it, Harold?" Max asked as kindly as he could.

The boy shook his head. "It was an accident." He started to walk away.

"An accident?" Max said, grabbing his arm. The picture in the newspaper floated into his mind. "What kind of accident?"

The boy pulled his arm free. His little cupid mouth opened and the words flowed out in a sing-song just on the edge of cracking. "You have to know what kind of girl she was."

"Wait," Max said. Some people passed them, a woman with a little boy and a man, all holding hands and swinging the little boy in the air as they walked. The little boy giggled with delight. Max and Harold started walking. Like father and son, Max thought. In another block they could see the Pacific Ocean, hear it crashing against the cliffs below. "She wasn't your girlfriend then?" Max asked.

"No. I knew who she was. Some of my friends used to talk about her. Well, I had nothing to do that night. All my friends had dates and I was just hanging around, tired of watching television, so I went out for a walk and I saw her sitting by herself in that hamburger place on Geary." They could see the ocean now as it ran up on the beach and slid back, but it was a long climb down. Harold had to raise his voice. "I never did anything like that before. I mean, I haven't gone out with a girl since I was sixteen and got acne. It's getting better now, though." He turned his face to show Max. "I've been taking care of it." Suddenly he pounded his fist into his thigh. "I asked her how come she didn't have a date. She said she just had one. Then she went into all sorts of detail about how this guy—" He looked at Max and then away. "—made love to her like. So I said would she go out with me. She said sure. She let me pay for her hamburger and then we walked around a little, talking about school and people we knew. I thought we would go to her place, but she said no, her parents were home, and we couldn't go to my place because of my mother, so I suggested the park."

Down below the waves assaulted the cliffs. "Go on!"

"So there we were kissing and fooling around and I thought this time for sure. Because, Mister, I never did that with a girl. All my friends did. At least they said they did. Some said they did it with her. I started to push her down, you know, and she said no she was tired from the other guy and pushed me away and I pushed her back."

Max grabbed the boy by the shoulders. "Go on!"

The boy pulled away and seemed to crumple like discarded wrapping paper. "She fell, I guess, and I got on top of her and when she didn't resist I thought she changed her mind and I started to pull at her underpants. Then I heard her moan and I saw blood oozing from her neck. I jumped up. Then I think I said her name and shook her. When she didn't say anything, I picked her head up a bit and there was a broken beer bottle under it. I pulled part of it away from her and there was even more blood."

"Then what did you do?"

"I started to run for help and then I saw you in the path

and I got scared and ran away."

He was crying now and on his knees, his hands folded in supplication.

"Get up," Max said. "Get up!" he shouted, looking frantically around the street. He pulled the boy to his feet and for a moment they stood face to face, breathing each other's breath.

"I'm sorry," Harold said. He took out a handkerchief and wiped his eyes.

"Don't rub."

Max did not know what to do. He put his arm around the boy's shoulders. All the things he wanted to say about justice and responsibility stuck in his throat like lumps of dry bread.

"They say she was raped. I didn't even.. We struggled, but I never..." The boy's hands fluttered like moths. "I didn't mean to hurt her. When I heard about it on the radio the next day I thought I would go crazy." He was shaking in Max's arm and bobbing back and forth the way old men do when they pray. "I went to church but I couldn't bring myself to confess. I couldn't even go to her funeral because I was afraid. Aw, shit!" He pulled himself free.

"Listen," Max said, "if you tell all this to the police I'm sure they would understand."

"Are you kidding? I would get the gas chamber for sure. Maybe it's what I deserve, but I don't want to die. I'm sorry for what I did, but I don't want to die or rot in jail for the rest of my life neither." His eyes widened and he squeezed hard on Max's arm. "You're not going to turn me in, are you? You wouldn't do that!"

"But you didn't kill her."

"Who will believe me? They'll say I hit her with it. That's why I went back later and got the part with my fingerprints on it. That was smart, wasn't it?"

"But they have arrested another man," Max said, pulling his arm free. "Don't you understand? Someone else will go to prison in your place. Or, maybe even be executed. What am I saying?"

"Let him," Harold said, turning away. "I'll never do anything like that again, I swear."

"But," Max said. His mouth was crammed with words struggling to get out. "Why should he suffer?"

"Look," the boy said, turning back again and staring Max in the face, "you're Jewish, aren't you?"

Max hesitated and then acknowledged that he was.

"Well, I saw where the guy they got was a Nazi. He must hate Jews. Look at what they did to your people in Germany. That's what he would do here if he got the chance. Why should you worry about him?"

Max shook his head. He wanted to remind the boy that Holtz after all was innocent, but he couldn't make himself say it.

"Promise you won't tell on me," the boy pleaded.

"I'll think about it," Max said. "No promises, but I'll think about it."

Silence spread between them as the boy backed away. Max was aware of the ocean again, crashing away down below. The boy's mouth opened and seemed to form the word *please*, though Max did not hear it, and then the boy walked swiftly away. He paused to look back once and then ran.

Nu? Max said to himself. Now what?

It was a long walk back to his room.

9

The boy's story paralyzed Max. He could neither turn the boy over to the police nor let Holtz die for the boy's crime. When the alarm went off in the morning, he lay in bed, letting it ring. Once he lifted an arm to stop it, but he could no more stop the alarm than he could stop the massive headache that throbbed in his temple and he let his arm drop. It was not until the alarm exhausted itself and the bell was silent that Max dragged himself from the bed. He took two aspirins before he brushed his teeth and then, unable to remember whether he had taken any or not, he took two more. It seemed as if all his blood had left his head, as if even his nerves and muscles were gone in order to leave more room for the headache. Next his bones would retract; he could feel them now beginning to tele-scope.With some effort he reached the kitchen chair and sat down. With all his blood and nerves and muscles gone from his head he could not remember what day of the week it was. It was a weekday. He knew that because of the alarm, so it didn't matter very much, but he did want to know. If it was a weekday, it occurred to him, he would have to go to work. He cleaned his glasses and then, con-centrating very hard on his heavy legs, he managed to stand up and put the water on for coffee. He drank some juice and put an egg on to fry too before he was exhaust-ed and had to sit down again.

Then he believed he saw the boy, Harold, in the room. "What do you want from me?" Max asked him. "Go pick on someone else." He stood up to confront the boy, but when he did the boy vanished. Max looked around the room. He was not sure why he had stood up, but he got dressed and drank the coffee, leaving the egg in the pan, but remembering to turn off the stove. He knew there was someone else he should think of and with a tremendous concentration he remembered Holtz. "But what is Holtz to me?" he asked the fading flowers on the wallpaper of his room.

He stood on his feet until his insides were back where they belonged and he knew what day it was. He could feel the bones settle into place, the blood beginning to flow again. Dizzy from the change, he went downstairs and found the Thompsons waiting for him.

"Are you all right?" the old woman asked.

Max looked puzzled. "Yes," he said. He started to nod, but this stirred up the headache so he only added, "I'm fine."

The Thompsons looked at each other. "We heard your alarm ring for a long time. I thought something might have happened."

"I told her not to meddle," the old man said. "A fine thing if she burst into your room and you were getting dressed or something." Mr. Thompson looked triumphantly at his wife.

"You do look a little pale," Mrs. Thompson said.

Max felt he would faint if he did not get out of there, but the old man had the stairs blocked. "I'm all right I tell you," he said, coming down another step.

"Well," Mr. Thompson said, moving aside, "looks like you will be late to work." Max looked at his watch, but it had stopped again. "Yes," he said. He came down to the landing and went all the way to the front door before he looked back and said: "Thank you."

"You just let us know if we can do anything for you," Mrs. Thompson called.

Max tried to hurry, but when he ran for the bus the headache joggled around like some palpable, weighty thing, so he walked lightly and as fast as he could on just the balls of his feet. He reached the office almost half an hour late, but the receptionist didn't take any notice of it. Shmuel, however, dropped a basket full of mail. "What's the matter with you?" he cried.

"What's the matter with you?" Max replied, easing himself into his chair.

"You look terrible. You're white like a ghost."

"Pick up your mail, Shmuel." He began to arrange the day's folders, but when he looked up and saw Shmuel on the floor, gathering up the mail, he said, "I was late so I was running."

This was the week before Shmuel's vacation. Max had forgotten that, but Shmuel reminded him later that day, saying, "I was thinking this year of going to Carmel- by-the- Sea. You know any good restaurants there?" Max groaned; with everything else he had to worry about, he would have to do Shmuel's job for two weeks. He always found this work degrading. Max felt his own job was bad enough; he could not understand anyone like Shmuel who was content to spend his days opening envelopes and mailing other peoples' letters. When Shmuel first came to the Agency Max almost resigned. Shmuel took over for a college student who held the job for the summer. Max discussed books and philosophy with the student and it was almost like being back in the university. In those days Max brought his lunch to work and they played chess during the lunch hour and again during the afternoon break, sometimes calling moves to each other while they worked in games that might last all week and have the social workers coming in to check every once in a while to see who was winning. Then the student went back to school and Shmuel came and held the job ever since. Shmuel read nothing but newspapers and though he claimed to be a chess player, Max beat him every game and soon the social workers in the next office lost interest and Max did also, sweeping the pieces to the floor one day and telling Shmuel he was a lousy player. He refused to play with him again. He even stopped bringing his lunch to work because Shmuel insisted on bringing jars of foul-smelling pickled herring which he ate in the office, mopping up the juice with slices of *challah*. During Passover Shmuel sometimes brought cream cheese or egg salad sandwiches on *matzoh*, grinning and shrugging his shoulders as the *matzoh* crumbled noisily and settled on his shirt and lap. And Shmuel wanted to talk Yiddish until Max had to pretend he didn't understand it in order to make Shmuel speak English. It was for his own good, Max said. How else would Shmuel learn the language? One day Max went to Dr. Resnick and asked him to get someone else. "It's him or me," Max said, but Dr. Resnick made him promise to give Shmuel a chance. Since then they worked together, but they never saw each other outside the office, so no one could have been more surprised than Max when Shmuel came to visit him.

It was Friday night. Max had spent the week thinking alternately about Holtz and Harold, trying to find a way out, until exhausted and feeling as if he had spent the week with the innocent Nazi and the guilty boy on his back, he lay down early praying he would fall asleep. There was a knock on the door and Max jumped. The knock sounded again, timid, hesitant, one knock and then two more. Max looked wildly about the room. It could not be the Thompsons because they always rapped on the door and called his name so his first thought was the boy. Perhaps he has come to say he will surrender to the police after all.

But halfway to the door Max thought, What if Holtz has escaped and come looking for him? Then he remembered that Holtz had never heard of him. The knock sounded once more. "Who's there?" Max asked the door.

"Just me," Shmuel said.

"What do you want, Shmuel?" Max opened the door a crack. Shmuel was standing not outside the door but one step down so that Max looked right over him at first and, thinking it had been his imagination, was about to close the door when Shmuel climbed back to the top step and said, "Good evening."

Max opened the door wider and stared at Shmuel whose wrinkled face looked not at Max but past him into the room. "Come in already," Max said.

Inside the room, Max hurried to take his shirt off the straight-backed chair, but he was too late. Shmuel was already seating himself in the easy chair by the bed and Max had to take the straight back chair himself and watch Shmuel sink into his favorite chair like a bird settling into its nest.

"It's a nice little place you got here," Shmuel said.

"How did you know where I live?"

"It's a secret?" Shmuel said, continuing to examine the room as if he were thinking of buying it. "Near the Park too," he said, nodding toward the window, though the Park was not in that direction.

Max wondered what he was getting at. "Is that what you came to tell me?" he asked.

Shmuel sank back farther in the chair and placed his hands on his thighs. "I was thinking today," he said, looking at the ceiling, "what do I need with two weeks vacation?"

"I don't understand."

"I don't know even what to do with one week."

"So?"

"So I was thinking, why don't you take one of my weeks?" Shmuel slapped his hands on his thighs as if he had just concluded a big deal.

Max got up and came to take a closer look at him. "What, are you crazy, Shmuel?" But he went to the kitchen and started water boiling for coffee. "Why do you want to do such a thing?" he asked.

"Well, you look like you can use a little more vacation," Shmuel said. "All week your face has been white as a sheet."

"I feel fine." Max was about to sit down again, but instead he stretched his arms wide and took a deep breath. It made him dizzy.

"Anyway," Shmuel said, "you're younger than I am. Take another week. Enjoy it."

Max did not know what to say. For one moment he saw himself in England but he quickly dismissed that, knowing he could not accept such a thing from Shmuel. No, he told himself, Shmuel is after something. He busied himself preparing the coffee, waiting for Shmuel to speak. When he could no longer bear the silence, Max asked, "What do you want, Shmuel?"

Shmuel put his finger tips together and then pulled them apart. "You don't know what I want, Max?" he said, leaning forward in the chair and raising a finger. Max waited, but then Shmuel sat back again without saying anything, pushing himself all the way into the chair so that only the tips of his shoes touched the floor. Shmuel is wiser than he looks, Max thought. He wondered if Shmuel knew anything about the park. He would have to be careful. The water whistled in the kettle and interrupted his thoughts, but as he finished preparing the coffee he kept an eye on Shmuel. He brought a cup of coffee to him.

"No, thank you," Shmuel said.

"You don't want coffee?"

"I never drink it."

"Why did you let me make it?"

"I didn't see what you were doing."

Max took the cup back and poured the coffee in the sink. "You want tea?" he asked, angrily.

"No, thanks."

"What do you want then?" Max yelled, brandishing his own cup and spilling the hot coffee on his hand. He would have cried if it weren't for Shmuel sitting across the room and watching him like a rabbi.

"Max, how many years have we worked together?"

"What?" Max yelled, struggling to make sense of Shmuel's question. "What difference does it make?"

"Just that it's time you treated me like I was human. I never said anything before, but it hurts, Max, believe me. Maybe you don't realize." He spoke so quietly that Max had to come close to hear him and when he understood he cried, *"What? What?"* in a voice that echoed faintly off the walls.

Shmuel went on talking. "I didn't want to say anything at the office with Resnick and everybody around, but tonight I made up my mind to tell you."

"What do you want me to do?" Max looked about the room, trying to find a way to escape. For a moment he considered going out and leaving the room to Shmuel, perhaps never returning.

"I don't say you have to go to parties with me," Shmuel said, his eyes following Max, "just you should say hello sometimes in the morning when you come to work, or maybe ask if I had a good lunch when you come back from the restaurant you go to so you shouldn't have to eat with me."

"You're crazy," Max told him, holding his hands over his ears.

Shmuel rolled back his sleeve and stood up to show Max the blue numbers tattooed on his forearm. Max turned away. "Look!" Shmuel said, shouting for the first time. "I was inside the wire not outside. Why do you treat me like I was a Nazi?"

Max went to the window and stared at the empty street. "I don't treat you like you were a—. You're being ridiculous, Shmuel. You hear?" He tried to wipe the tears from his eyes without Shmuel seeing. He didn't know how they got there. "Get out!" he yelled over his shoulder. "Get out!"

"*Inside!*" Shmuel yelled. "*We were both inside!*"

"Get out, Shmuel. I don't want to hear anymore." He heard Shmuel get up. For more than a minute there was no sound in the room. His entire body trembling, Max turned around. Shmuel was gone.

Later, while his milk warmed on the stove and he was getting undressed, he thought: *As if I didn't have enough troubles. First a murderer and now that lousy Polack.*

10

Max stared at the pile of mail sitting unfamiliarly on his own desk. He filed and refiled the last of Friday's folders before taking the first envelope from the pile and shaking it so he would not slice the letter in two as Shmuel sometimes did. He wondered if he should tell Dr. Resnick about Shmuel's visit. What if Shmuel never came back? Max measured the envelope against the letter opener and made a quick, clean slit, extracting the letter and pressing out its creases. Across the room Shmuel's vacant desk seemed to accuse him of something and Max remembered Shmuel asking *Why do you treat me like I was a Nazi?* He resisted the temptation to roll back his sleeve and look at the numbers on his own arm.

At ten o'clock Dr. Resnick looked in, glancing first at Shmuel's desk and then at Max still opening the mail. "Anything for me?" he asked.

Max looked through the stack of opened letters and handed one to him. He started to look through the unopened mail and the psychiatrist said, "I didn't mean to rush you."

Max found another letter for him. Didn't mean to rush me, Max thought as the psychiatrist left. He doesn't have to sit here opening letters like a trained ape. In a few minutes Resnick was back. He smoked a pipe and when he talked he held the pipe in his hand like a begging bowl. "I hate to rush you," he said, "but is there anything new for the Goldman file? He's in my office now."

Max went through the letters again and found one to give him. He had not had time to read it and now he would probably not find out if Goldman's missing wife had been found until the case was completed and the folder came back to him. It was the most interesting case that had developed since Max returned from Los Angeles and he felt cheated. If Shmuel had been there he would have opened the letter and brought it over, saying, "Here's a letter from the police in New Orleans. It must be about Goldman's wife."

The next day the secretary asked him if he wanted the mail put on his desk or on Shmuel's. "Put it on Shmuel's desk," he said, and when she left he gathered it up and brought it to his own desk. But the next week he found himself opening the mail at Shmuel's desk and thinking, Here I am in Shmuel's place. Then he wondered, What would Shmuel do if he were in my place? The idea fascinated him. He hunched down in the chair and tried to imagine that he was Shmuel. "Here's a letter from Mr. Schneider," Max said, stroking his chin until he remembered that Shmuel did not have a beard. Then he closed his eyes and tried to imagine that he was Shmuel in the park that night when the boy jumped out of the bushes. He knew what Shmuel would have done. He would have run away and there would have been no dilemma. But suppose he hadn't? Suppose he remembered the boy's face and knew that the man they arrested wasn't guilty, what then? Max stood up and tried to walk like Shmuel. Probably he would do nothing, Max decided. He wouldn't want to get involved. Or else he would come to me for advice. Max minced over to his own desk and imitated Shmuel's confidential voice. "Help me, Max," he whispered to the empty chair. "I got a problem." *And I would tell him... I would say,* "Look here, Shmuel."

Dr. Resnick came in and stared at Max crouched before his own desk. Max quickly bent the rest of the way to the floor and tied his shoelace.

"Sorry to bother you," Dr. Resnick said, lighting his pipe. "I just came in to see if you could spare some empty folders. I'm fresh out in there."

Max got the folders out of the supply cabinet. He knew his face was red and he could feel the psychiatrist's eyes at his back. Why doesn't he knock before he comes in?

"Would you miss Shmuel if he didn't come back?" the psychiatrist asked, accepting the folders.

"Has anything happened to him?"

"Not that I know of," Dr. Resnick said, fixing his gaze on Shmuel's empty desk. "What makes you think something happened to him?"

Feeling that he had been trapped into some kind of game, Max said loudly, "Because of the way you ask if I would miss him, like you just heard he had been killed or something."

"Oh no," Dr. Resnick laughed. He examined the bowl of his pipe and in his soft monotone said, "I was just remembering that you once wanted me to fire him. I'm glad the two of you get along now." He saluted with his pipe and returned to his own office. The sweet smell of the psychiatrist's pipe tobacco hung in the air. Max opened a window and angrily fanned the last wisps of smoke that Dr. Resnick had left behind.

When Shmuel returned to work the following Monday, Max asked him if he enjoyed his vacation. "It was all right," Shmuel said. He looked tanned and relaxed in a new tweed suit and a bright green tie with oranges painted on it that hung long and wide like a sick and displaced tongue. Max could not bring himself to mention the new outfit. He did not know they made ties like that anymore.

"I went to Carmel for a few days," Shmuel was saying while Max's eyes wrestled with the tie, "but I didn't like it. Too pink and fancy for my tastes, so I came back and treated myself to a new suit instead. You like it? Then I spent the rest of the time at Aquatic Park getting a little sun when it was out. I told you, I don't know what to do with vacations."

As Shmuel talked, a strange idea crept through Max's mind: if he could not let Holtz die, and he could not turn the boy in, then maybe he could find a substitute-Shmuel, for instance!

Just then Dr. Resnick came in to welcome Shmuel back to work. "I see you got a new suit," he said.

Shmuel got up to show off the suit.

"Very nice," the psychiatrist said, turning to smile at Max.

Or Dr. Resnick, Max thought, slowly returning the psychiatrist's smile. As soon as Dr. Resnick left, the idea collapsed like a punctured balloon and Max wondered if he were going crazy. But all day, whenever he looked up and saw Shmuel sitting behind his desk, Max pictured him strapped to the chair in the gas chamber at San Quentin and he had to shake his head to dismiss the picture.

"Is something wrong?" Shmuel asked once.

"What do you mean?"

"You keep shaking your head like you got fleas or something."

Max did not answer.

That afternoon, when he was leaving work, a woman was arguing with the receptionist. "Try an employment agency," the receptionist said, and the woman in exasperated tones said, "I've been to twenty employment agencies already. That's why I came here." Max said goodbye to the receptionist and went out, but before he was halfway down the block he heard a voice cry "Mister! Wait, Mister." He turned and saw the woman hurrying after him.

Although there was no possibility of rain, she was waving an umbrella as she ran.

Max waited nervously. When she caught up to him she had to catch her breath before she could speak. "You work there?" she said, pointing back at the agency with her umbrella. Max said he did. "Maybe you can help me." A bird's nest of gray hair crowned her head and in the tense features of her face a pair of soft blue eyes looked up and pleaded with him.

"What is the trouble?" Max asked.

"I need a job." She brought the point of the umbrella down on the sidewalk.

"But we're not an employment agency," Max said quickly before she could say anything else. "We help with family problems."

"This is a family problem," she said, brushing back a stray wisp of hair. "That's what I tried to explain to the receptionist. My husband died two years ago. I should have looked for work then but I didn't and now the insurance money is running out. My boy wants to go to college, but either he has to go to work or I have to, so I'm looking for a job so my son can get an education. Isn't that a family problem?"

Leaning on the umbrella and gesturing with one hand, she looked so reasonable that Max did not know how to answer her. For a moment he considered going back to the office to tell Dr. Resnick about her case, but he finally admitted to her that he was only a clerk. "I just file papers. I can't help you. I'm sorry."

She said, "Oh," and they both stood facing each other for a moment, Max shuffling his feet and the woman touching her hair. Then Max turned and walked toward the bus stop. He heard footsteps behind him, but he did not look back until he got to the corner. She smiled and with her hand indicated that this was her bus stop too. She lived just a few blocks away from Max and on the bus she turned to him and said, "You're from Austria?" Max shook his head. "That's what I thought," she said, sighing deeply and folding her hands in her lap.

"I'm from Germany," Max said. "From Berlin."

She looked out the window. "I knew. I could tell."

Max was bewildered; he felt he had to explain further so he said, "I didn't get out until after the war."

She touched his arm. "You don't have to tell me."

When they got off the bus Max started to say goodbye, but she pointed out the direction in which she lived and Max walked along beside her, wondering if he should offer to carry her umbrella.

"What kind of work were you looking for?" he asked.

"Anything. I worked once in a library and before that in a nursery school, but that was a long time ago. I can't type, which is the only kind of work anyone seems to want. I've even been to the restaurants to find work as a cook. I'm a pretty good cook." They were passing a fast food restaurant and she made a face to show that in there they did not know anything about cooking.

When they got to her house, a five-story apartment house that leaned on the shoulders of the houses on either side, Max slowed down. She pointed towards one of the upper floors. "That's where I live. come to see me some time. Don't be bashful, Mister"

"Friedman," Max said. "Max Friedman."

"Clara Axelrod here." She turned and was gone before Max could say goodbye.

Walking back along Geary Boulevard, Max thought, It's too bad a woman like that has to go out and find a job at her age. He passed the fast food restaurant. He had eaten there several times and had meant to tell her they made good hamburgers. Max crossed the street. "What is the trouble?" he said aloud, testing his accent. He wondered how she knew where he was from.

Summer was almost over now. When he was young, Max liked autumn best of all. He would take long walks in the country and when he was very young and not allowed to walk by himself down country roads, he would walk around his own block. When the leaves were raked in big piles like red and yellow stars fallen to Earth he and his friends would jump and play in them until someone came to chase them away, cursing them for having scattered the leaves. One autumn Max collected as many different colors of leaves as he could find. But the seasons did not change in San Francisco and Shmuel's return from his vacation was the surest sign Max had that summer was coming to an end. Downtown there were not as many tourists and the pace of things seemed somehow a bit quicker and soon it would rain. Max walked along the wide street, kicking aside pieces of paper and wondering what happened to his leaf collection. He could not remember throwing it away, but he supposed it could not have survived the war.

11

Max tore August off the calendar and stared at the empty succession of days ahead. For an innocent man in prison in the Hall of Justice, time was running out and Max held the key or, rather, the button. He didn't laugh at his joke; he only wondered if Holtz too stared at the calendar. The noise of a car horn took his mind off Holtz and drew him to the window where he saw a couple he recognized as friends of the Thompsons getting out of a car. Mr. Thompson, wearing only a bathing suit, bounced out to meet them and Max heard Mrs. Thompson calling him back in while the couple laughed and waved their hands. Then they were all in the house and Max heard the laughter continue downstairs. He pulled down the shade, but it popped back up. He pulled it down again and the bright shards of sunlight melted and turned the room to shadow. Fragments of laughter drifted up through the stairwell. If they were not gone before he had to leave for work, he swore he would look for another place to live.

"Mr. Friedman, are you there?" Mrs. Thompson called up the stairs.

Max, sitting on the edge of the bed and waiting to go to work, stirred and rested his chin on his fist.

"Can I come up, Mr. Friedman?"

Hearing her steps on the staircase, Max went to the door and asked her what she wanted.

"I just wanted to tell you we are going to Stinson Beach for a few days. We won't be back until late Friday." She wore a large straw bonnet and a pink sunsuit. Behind her, Mr. Thompson appeared. He was just putting on a sportshirt that was patterned with rainbows, each one ending in a pot of gold. "How do you like it?" he called to Max. His wife pushed him back towards the living room, saying, "Put your pants on and let's go." He managed to wink at Max before he was out of sight.

Max went back to sit on the bed and wait. Presently he heard four voices shout, "Goodbye Mr. Friedman!" He waited a few minutes more and then hurried for the bus.

When Dr. Resnick stepped into the office Max remembered to tell him about Clara Axelrod. He took the psychiatrist out to the reception room so Shmuel would not hear, but the receptionist had already told the story and after a few words Dr. Resnick said, "I'm sorry. You know we can't find jobs for people. Do you know this woman?"

"Oh, no," Max said. "She stopped me on the street yesterday and I told her the same thing." He went back to his folders telling himself that he hadn't promised her anything, but feeling that he had failed.

That night he sat in his room watching it grow dark. Without the occasional footsteps of the Thompsons and the muffled sound of the television as if a drama were taking place in his closet, the house seemed lonely. The voices of his mind began a conversation. The first one said: *It's too bad Dr. Resnick didn't have any suggestions about where that woman could find a job, you could go visit her.* And the second voice replied: It wouldn't hurt to take a walk.

Max walked down Geary Boulevard until he reached the corner where Clara Axelrod lived; there he hesitated, then walked another block. *What are you going to do*, the first voice said, *knock on her door and tell her the agency doesn't find jobs for people?* He turned around and walked back, pausing to look down the stone gray void of her street and then hurried home.

The night was dark and soft as a black cat and for a long time Max sat by the open window and watched the stars edge their way across the sky. He remembered how one night he and Sarah sat on a bench deep in the Tiergarten and counted the stars. She found more than he did. They kissed and talked until the moon had gone from one horizon to the other and then they returned home, Max watching as Sarah sneaked quietly into her house and then going home as dawn began to swallow the sky. Now Sarah was up there among the stars.

He remembered that he was alone in the house and he went downstairs where there was room to pace around. It was strange to find the house so dark and quiet: In the living room he thought he could feel the china animals watching him, resenting his presence. As if to defy them, he turned on the television set and sat down in Mrs. Thompson's chair. The news was on and he intended to go to bed as soon as it was over, but the chair was so comfortable that he stayed to watch the beginning of the movie that followed and then he fell asleep. When he awoke only a spot of light like a roving eye came from the television set along with a humming sound. Max turned off the set and dragged himself upstairs.

In the morning, when the alarm went off, he opened his eyes but did not dare move his head for the pain that pressed with the force of a steamroller against his forehead. Wisps of gray fog floated into the room and he lay in bed and cursed himself for forgetting to close the window. Each breath was a separate effort, like drawing water from a well; he hoarded air in his lungs like a miser, saving it up until he could turn off the alarm and get up to shut the window. Fog billowed like dragon's breath in the street. He made a cup of coffee and took two aspirin with it and then he got dressed and went to work, every movement of his head producing a whip of pain.

He sat at his desk and held his head. It felt as if it were turning to stone. Shmuel watched. "Your sinuses?" he asked. Max started to nod, but the headache held him back.Shmuel brought the mail over and then stood at Max's desk until Max asked him what he wanted.

"Try bending way over with your head between your knees," Shmuel advised.

"That's for hiccups."

"For hiccups?" Shmuel looked puzzled. "You're sure?"

"Go away," Max said. "Leave me alone already." That's the kind of help I get, he thought, but a little later, when Shmuel left the room to deliver the mail, Max tried bending over as far as he could. It didn't help.

By the afternoon the pain was not as bad; it had become a fist, flexing and unflexing, but he could bear it. Still, a headache had never lasted so long. It was still there when he went home. Lunch had made him nauseous and he was trying to decide what to have for dinner when he found among the bills and magazines that had come for the Thompsons a letter for himself. It was not from his cousin in Los Angeles and it did not appear to be an advertisement. He tore it open.

Sept. 1

Dear Mr. Friedman:

I am leaving home. By the time you read this I will be far away and not even my parents will know where I have gone. I am sorry for what I did and I know I should give myself up like you said only I am afraid to. Besides, I have thought about it a long time and I hope they do not execute the man they

*have accused of my crime, but if they do then it is
him or me and I feel that I have more to live for. At
least I am not a nazi. I will get a new start in life
where I am going and maybe some day I can make
up for what I did. I could not make up for it if I was
dead or in prison. Thank you for not turning me in.
I will always be grateful.*

*Very truly yours,
Harold Kirby*

"*But Holtz didn't do it!*" Max shouted at the letter. The
pain flowered suddenly, filling his head, and Max sat
down and cried, but as he sat wiping tears from his cheeks,
something in him wished the boy good luck. It occurred to
him then that somewhere in the city the boy's parents were
wondering where their son had gone. They will call the
police! At least Max knew why the boy ran away; his parents would not even know that, and Max felt sorry for
them. He felt like a sort of secret godfather until, like an
accusing finger, it came to him that he had driven the boy
to run away. "Aach!" Max stared at his hands. The blood
was draining away from his fingers. He clenched his
hands and the nails dug into his palms like clenching
barbed wire. "But what could I have done?" He read the
letter over and then he tore it into little pieces and flushed
it down the toilet, thinking: So it will have to be the Nazi.
The fist flexed in his head and he wished there were someone to talk to.

He was somewhat calmer as he walked along Geary
Boulevard on his way to Clara Axelrod's house, thinking,
Why not? She said herself don't be bashful. First he
walked very quickly and then he slowed down to catch his
breath. When he stood outside her apartment the pain in
his head had reduced itself to a dull throb. Then he won-

dered if he should really be there, but his finger seemed to decide for him and he watched it ring the bell. At first there was no answer and he was about to leave when he heard Clara call "Who's there?"

Max took a deep breath. "Max Friedman. I don't know if you remember."

He heard her coming to the door, then going away from it, and then back again. The door opened. Clara was in a housecoat. "Come in," she said, her hands darting to her hair and her face like worried birds. "I look terrible. I wasn't expecting."

"I shouldn't have come."

"What are you saying? Come in." She took his arm and pulled him into the apartment, but then she ran into the bedroom. "Give me just a minute," she said. "Sit down. I'm glad you came."

Max sat down on the edge of the sofa. I shouldn't have come, he thought. I should at least have called. He took a chocolate from the box on the coffee table and ate it quickly, wondering if he should have brought a box of candy, but deciding, as he popped one more into his mouth, that it would not have looked right.

Clara was out of the room so long that Max began to worry. He was just about to knock on the bedroom door when she came out wearing a dress and smelling vaguely sweet. Max stepped back. "You look beautiful," he said. Clara waved her hand. She indicated the easy chair for Max and she sat on a straight back chair, her hands folded in her lap. For Max communication seemed to have gone to his hands; they fluttered and gestured, but he could not speak. Finally, he jumped up. "I shouldn't have bothered you. I'm sorry."

"Bothered?" Clara was up too. "I asked you to come."

Max sat down again. "I was in the neighborhood." *Of*

course you were in the neighborhood. You live three blocks away. "I wanted someone to talk to."

"Good. I was just in the mood for listening."

Just then the door opened and a tall boy with dark hair and black-rimmed glasses came in. Max had forgotten she had a son and he cursed himself again for coming. The boy did not see Max at first. He went to his mother and said hello and kissed her on her forehead. Max looked at the boy. In profile his face was very angular. A high sloping forehead rode over a ridge to his eyes and his nose seemed to have a joint in it. Even his chin looked like it came to a point, though Max saw on him the full lips of his mother. In fact, except that he must be a foot taller than Clara and thinner of course, he looked very much like her. "What's for supper?" he asked.

Clara stood up and turned him around to face Max. "I want you to meet Mister Friedman. He works at that Agency."

"Hello," the boy said, looking around to see if anyone else was there.

"This is my boy, Arnold."

Max said hello. He would have said more, but Clara was pushing Arnold into the bedroom and Max was left alone again. Clara stuck her head out for a moment to say, "Excuse us."

Not only did I barge in, Max thought, but I came right at dinner time. When they came back in the room, Max got up to leave, but before he could say anything the boy went past him, paused at the door to say, "Nice to have met you," and was out of the apartment.

"That was a short visit," Max said.

Clara laughed. "He just remembered he was supposed to eat at a friend's house. Now what am I going to do with the blintzes?"

"Blintzes?"

"I suppose you've eaten already?"

"To tell you the truth I forgot to eat dinner tonight."

"Well, it's a lucky thing you came," she said, "or I would have had to eat alone. You can't keep a teenager in the house."

By the time he had finished eating, Max agreed it was lucky he had come. He hadn't had blintzes like that since he was a child. Sarah always burned them, or made them too greasy, until she gave up making them altogether. Only his mother made blintzes like this, he told Clara. She clasped her hands and thanked him. "Thank me?" he said. "Thank you, Mrs. Axelrod." She asked him to call her Clara.

Later, after Max insisted on helping her with the dishes, they sat in the living room and talked.

"It's all true what we heard about the concentration camps?"

Max nodded.

"Don't tell me the details," she said.

"I wouldn't tell such things to a woman like you." And while she shook her head and sighed he quickly asked her where she was from.

"I was born in New York." She described Washington Heights when she was a girl and then the years she had spent in The Bronx before she married and moved to San Francisco. She loved San Francisco, the beautiful hills, the climate that was always autumn, the different colors of the city. "Only now there's no one to talk to."

"How about Arnold?"

"Did you ever try to talk to a teenager?"

Max thought of Harold, but he shook his head. "No, I guess I haven't," he said. Then, when silence threatened, he asked her if she liked the fog.

"Yes, I even like the fog," she said. It reminded her of the women in Baltimore she heard about who came out every Saturday morning to clean the steps.

"It gives me headaches," Max said. He told her about the headache he had all day. It had gone away for a while, but talking about it brought it back and he could feel it lurking behind his eyes. "But there's no fog now," she told him. Max glanced at the window. It had turned gray with evening, but there was no fog. "Just a little in the morning is enough to give me a headache all day long."

"You poor man," Clara said. "My late husband used to get headaches like that too. He liked me to rub his forehead." And before Max knew what she was doing, she was sitting on the arm of his chair rubbing her cool fingers over his forehead. He wanted to look around, to go home, but she was right. The headache retreated before her fingers. When he glanced at the window again, it was black with night. What am I doing? he asked himself. I just came to talk. He jumped up and put on the light. "Someone might get the wrong idea," he explained, pointing to the black window.

"I'll make some coffee," Clara said.

Max paced the living room. He remembered that he had come to ask her about the boy and the Nazi, but that seemed far away now; besides, he didn't want to appear involved. Still, he wondered what she thought about it and when she came in with the coffee he said, "You remember that man they arrested for the murder in Golden Gate Park?"

Clara thought a minute. "No," she said. "I don't remember."

Max described some of the details to her. "They arrested this Holtz. They say he's a Nazi."

"Oh, yes. I read about it."

"What do you think about it?" Max asked, sipping the coffee and watching her over the rim of the cup.

"What do I think? He rapes and murders a young girl and on top of that he's a Nazi? Let them hang him."

"Gas," Max said.

"What?"

"Gas. They don't hang in California. They use gas."

"So let them use gas."

"But suppose he didn't do it?"

Clara sipped her coffee. "Why do you ask? You know him?"

"No," Max said. "I was just wondering. Should we kill him just because he's a Nazi?" "Didn't they kill Jews just because they were Jews?"

Max shrugged. He didn't want to talk about it anymore; he was afraid he already said too much. He finished his coffee and said he would go.

"Come again," Clara said. "Please."

"I will. I promise." He took her hand and almost kissed it.

Walking home he thought: So the boy and Clara both agree, Holtz should be punished for what he might do. If only he could believe that, everything would be so much easier. He told himself that Holtz would not mind seeing Jews killed. But that's just it, he thought. If Holtz has to be punished, let him be punished for what he does, not for what he might do. Otherwise, how are we better than the Nazis? He thought it over several times while sitting on the edge of the bed, waiting for the milk to warm up. Why me, he thought. Why do I have to be caught in the middle? But at least Clara's fingers had taken his headache away.

12

The man sitting next to Max on the bus asked him to be quiet. "I didn't say anything," Max said. "You were humming," the man said. "Was I?" Max asked. He listened back over the last few minutes and realized that he had been humming. "I'm sorry," he said, and he did not start humming again until he arrived at the office.

Shmuel was not there. Max hummed a while and then sat down and began to tap his fingers on the desk. Soon he stopped humming and just tapped his fingers. He was about to ask Dr. Resnick what happened to Shmuel when the psychiatrist came in.

"Shmuel just called. He's taking the morning off to attend a funeral. Would you mind opening the mail today?"

"A funeral?" Max asked. "Who died?"

"He didn't say." Dr. Resnick's brow wrinkled and stretched again. "It was probably a friend. I don't think he had any close relatives left."

The psychiatrist turned to go, but Max asked, "Why didn't he say something yesterday?"

"He said he forgot. That's why I don't imagine it was anyone too close to him."

Dr. Resnick left and Max went over to Shmuel's desk to open the mail. How could he forget a funeral? Max wondered. He bit his lip as the memory of Grandfather Mordecai's funeral rushed in upon him. He remembered staring at the plain pine coffin, trying to picture his Grandfather resting in there. Afterwards, some boys were waiting outside the funeral home and they laughed and pointed when the coffin was brought out. One of Max's uncles chased them away, but they came back even before everyone was in the cars. And at home the house was very quiet. Though many people came to console the family, they all spoke in whispers. Max's father had torn the lapel of his suit and he sat on a wooden orange crate and said prayers most of the day, but Max could hear his parents in the next room at night and the first night after the funeral he heard his mother say, "I bet I know who did it. I'm going to tell the police," and his father answered: "Don't make trouble. We got enough." And his aunts and uncles came and they said, "We told him not to wear that ridiculous outfit." And except on the holidays the aroma of the sweet wine was gone from the house.

When Shmuel came back to work in the afternoon, Max told him he was sorry about the death.

"A cousin," Shmuel said. "A nice fellow." He shook his head and sighed. "I guess it comes to us all."

Later, Max looked up from his work and watched Shmuel. Bent over his desk, Shmuel might have been a rabbi, but his thin hands leafed through envelopes rather than Bible pages and where there should have been a skull cap there were only black hairs darting out in all directions as if waiting for a signal to depart. Something about Shmuel bent over his desk reminded Max of Grandfather Mordecai as he used to study his books in the evening. Of course Mordecai was almost twice Shmuel's size and was really nothing like him; still Max wondered if Shmuel's house smelled of sweet wine and egg bread.

It was time for Shmuel's break. Usually, Max would keep working. Shmuel would pour himself some tea from a thermos and then read the newspaper and sip tea with loud sucking noises while Max concentrated on the letters and applications before him, cursing unmannered Polacks

97

beneath his breath. Once Max had asked him if he couldn't make less noise when he drank and Shmuel had said yes, but he went right on making noise. Then, when Shmuel went back to work Max would take his break, eating a candy bar he bought at lunch and sometimes reading a magazine in the reception room or walking around the block if the weather were nice. But today when Shmuel poured his tea, Max stopped working too. He walked over to Shmuel's desk and put his hand on the newspaper before Shmuel could pick it up.

"Tell me, Shmuel," Max said. "Why do you call yourself Shmuel?"

Shmuel's eyes narrowed. He looked at Max's hand on the newspaper and he scratched his head. Finally he shrugged his shoulders like one who knows he is about to give the wrong answer to a riddle and said: "Because that's my name."

"But you're in America now," Max said. "You could call yourself Samuel."

"I could call myself George Washington, but my name is Shmuel."

Max stared at him a moment. He leaned over the desk and sniffed but smelled only lemon tea and the lunchtime odor of herring. "Never mind," Max said. Shmuel tugged at the newspaper and Max took his hand away.

Outside, the day was gray without fog and Max, standing in the doorway of the agency, could not decide whether or not to take a walk. He watched the children playing tag in the street. Next door a woman sat on the steps of her house and rocked a baby in her arms, vainly trying to quiet the children without waking her own child. Max grabbed a boy as he ran by. "Not so much noise," he said, pointing to the baby next door, but the boy squirmed out of Max's grasp and ran shouting across the street. Max opened his hands and let them drop to show the woman that he could not quiet them either. She nodded and went in the house. Max walked a few steps. *George Washington!* He laughed at the notion. *That Shmuel!* Then he wondered again what Shmuel would have done had he been in the Park that night. He couldn't tell him about the boy, but he had an idea and he went inside and stood before Shmuel's desk and cleared his throat until Shmuel looked up.

"Tell me, Shmuel," Max said as they peered at each other over the newspaper, "suppose you saw Doctor Resnick commit a crime and the police arrested for it a real no good, a Nazi. Would you tell the police it was Doctor Resnick that did it?"

"Resnick? The psychiatrist?" Shmuel asked, putting the paper down and inclining his head towards the consultation room.

"Yes. Would you report him? I mean, if it were a real crime. Say a murder."

"Resnick a murderer?"

"Yes," Max said loudly. "Just suppose."

"What is it with all the riddles today?" Shmuel asked, taking a noisy sip of tea but keeping his steady eyes on Max.

Max threw up his hands and walked all the way around the room. When he got back to Shmuel's desk he leaned over it. He could feel the warmth rise from the tea. "The other day you came to my house to tell me I didn't talk to you. Now I talk to you, you don't want to talk."

"Two weeks," Shmuel said, "not the other day. And who said I didn't want to talk? I just asked why all the riddles."

"You don't have to answer."

"I'm thinking." Shmuel sucked in some more tea and

scratched his head. His eyes seemed to leave the room and he screwed up his face and sat silent. Max waited. Finally, Shmuel said: "If you like apples and you don't like oranges, which would you rather have, a juicy orange or an apple with a worm in it?"

"What?"

"Which weighs more, a pound of lead or a pound of grapes?"

"You're some help," Max said, going back to his own desk.

"What do you mean?" Shmuel called after him. "Did Resnick really do something?"

"No, of course not."

"So then who needs help?"

"Never mind," Max said. It was what he could expect from Shmuel. He went back to work, knowing Shmuel was still looking at him as if he were crazy. For the rest of the afternoon he avoided Shmuel's eyes, but that evening, as he sliced onions for his dinner, it occurred to him that Shmuel was right. It was the balance that was the problem; if he could change that he would know what to do. If the boy, for example, were a habitual criminal, or if Holtz were, say, a Jew. He laughed at the idea and shoveled the onions into the pan of hot oil, but while he prepared the peas he thought, Why couldn't Holtz be a Jew? *What? Holtz? A Nazi you're going to make a Jew?* He dropped the liver in the pan and watched it jump and splutter. Still, he could be a Nazi and not an anti-Semite. Even in the camps there was more than one guard who had said "I have nothing against the Jews personally." If he could really convert Holtz, that would be something. But, ah, the idea was ridiculous. He warmed up some peas. I really must be going crazy, he thought. He set the table and soon burned his tongue on a fried onion.

Lying in bed that night he thought, It's not too late to turn the boy in. Max propped himself up on his elbow to look at the bureau where the button lay. If he could be sure the police would never find him, he would bring it to the station right now.

He dreamt of Holtz in his khaki uniform with a yellow Star of David sewn over the breast pocket and when he woke up a voice from some dark corner of his mind whispered, *Why not? There's nothing to lose by trying*, against a chorus that shouted *Ridiculous! Fantastic*!

At work he found himself thinking: sure, you just walk up to him in his cell and say, Holtz, you Nazi, how would you like to become Jewish? That was another problem. Memories of his last attempt to see Holtz suddenly kindled in him as he saw himself surrounded by marble walls. He shut out the picture, but after work curiosity drove him to the Hall of Justice.

Some people were picketing. They were young mostly and they wore black armbands and carried signs protesting capital punishment. One of the signs listed the people who awaited execution on San Quentin's Death Row: six men and one woman. One of the men was named Heinz and when Max looked at the sign he thought it said Holtz and his heart tripped. Frantically, he looked up at the barred windows on the top floor, but he could see nothing behind the bars and he started to race into the lobby when he glanced again at the sign and then again, swallowing the information: Heinz, not Holtz.

He wanted to go into the building anyway and ask again if he could see Holtz, though he knew it was no use. He wanted to go up to the blind newsstand man and ask him something to see if he remembered him. Standing on the sidewalk, facing the gray slab building, a line of pickets on one side of him and lawyers and visitors hurrying by him on the other side, Max felt foolish for coming. He turned to go just as one of the pickets asked him to sign a petition. "No, no," Max said, frightened and jumping out of the picket's reach. Another picket, a young woman this time with long red hair, offered him a leaflet. Max retreated another step. She held it out to him and Max took it and quickly put it in his pocket. Just then an older woman attacked the pickets. She brandished a wide brim hat and swatted at the pickets with it. "Trouble makers!" she shouted. "You want to let murderers roam the streets?" She knocked the leaflets from the young woman's hands; when they slid to the ground she kicked them back and forth along the street. One of the pickets stepped up to her, but she swatted him before he could speak. A crowd gathered now, men with briefcases and women with children. Most of them laughed. The old woman's white hair slipped from its pins and curls unraveled as she charged the picket line again. "Go home where you belong!"

A man pushed his way through the crowd and led the woman away. She menaced the pickets with her hat as he pulled at her arm. When they were gone, the pickets began picking up the leaflets. "Hold this, please," a young man said, thrusting a sign at Max and bending down to help pick up the leaflets. Max looked at the sign in his hands. It said: CAPITAL PUNISHMENT IS LEGAL MURDER. He looked at the people around him. The crowd was beginning to disperse, but one or two stopped to read his sign. Max's eyes waxed like two moons. He had never held a picket sign before.

13

Max woke up early with the sound of marching storm-boots echoing out of a dream, realized it was Saturday, and went back to sleep. An hour later he whispered Clara's name and woke up embracing the sunlight on his bed. He decided to call her. When he saw what time it was, he decided to call right away. He put on a bathrobe and went downstairs wondering what had made him sleep so late.

The Thompsons let him use the hall telephone. He had his own phone when he lived downtown but the only calls he ever got were from salesmen and solicitors so he gave it up. Perhaps she will invite me for dinner, he thought, as he balanced the telephone book on his knee. "Awson, Axedikian, Axel, Axelrod!" he muttered. He looked for a pencil and saw Mrs. Thompson coming out of the kitchen. She saw him at the same time and they both gasped. Max dropped the phone book, clutched his bathrobe around him and retreated up the stairs out of sight.

"Mr. Friedman, was that you?" Mrs. Thompson asked timidly.

"Yes, it's me," he said. "I thought you were in Stinson Beach."

"We came back last night. I didn't mean to frighten you."

"I'll get dressed," Max said.

"You can use the phone. I'm in the kitchen."

He would have to go out to call. "I was just looking something up, thank you," he said, hurrying to his room. If Mr. Thompson heard him talking to a woman, he would never hear the end of it.

At the drugstore he bought a newspaper to see if there was a movie or a concert he could ask her to, but sitting in the phone booth and looking through the entertainment section of the paper, he saw something that made him forget all about calling Clara.

Everyone Invited
Rally
Entertainment Dancing
Benefit
Mort Holtz Defense Committee
Wagner Hall
Tonight Saturday 8pm

The ad was set in the corner of the page, beneath the ads for concerts and lectures. It seemed personal somehow, a message directed at Max Friedman, as if it should have been in the personals section. He wondered why he had not heard of the Mort Holtz Defense Committee before. At least someone is trying to help him, he thought. Someone was waiting to use the phone. Max left the booth. His stomach reminded him that he had not had breakfast so he tore the ad out of the paper, carefully folded it and put it in his wallet, and took a seat at the drug store's lunch counter.

That evening he took a bus to Wagner Hall. He held the ad in his hand but he did not look at it; instead, his eyes swallowed the rows of slatted houses in this area of the city where he had never been before. It was a dark, deserted, ghost town of a neighborhood and Max wondered if it were wise to come. When he got off the bus he could smell

the Bay. He was all alone and he watched the bus dimin-
ish in the street and blink out like a candle.

Wagner Hall was over a grocery in a street of gray
houses and unlit stores. It was a few minutes after eight
when Max got there. An old couple hurried down the
street and up the stairs, the man waving to Max as they
went by. After their footsteps stopped resounding on the
wooden stairs, there was nothing to hear. Max bent low
and looked up the stairwell. At the top he could see a
square of light and a man's legs. There was a sudden mass
scraping of chairs and the sound of people getting to their
feet as a piano started playing "The Star Spangled
Banner" and everyone sang. Max took a deep breath and
climbed the stairs. The man at the head of the stairs was
tall with a crew cut and a narrow face. In one hand he held
an overseas cap and with the other he motioned Max to
wait and be still. Max stood on the top step. The man wore
the khaki uniform with the swastika armband. Max looked
at the man's feet. At least he wasn't wearing boots.

When the singing stopped the man at the door
motioned Max to come in. Max mounted the top step and
the man held a cigar box in front of him with a sign on it
that said: *Donation $5*. Max fumbled in his wallet and pro-
duced a five dollar bill which he dropped in the box.

The hall itself was a large room with green paint peeling from its wooden walls. On one side were two blind
windows; at the front, facing the rows of wooden chairs,
an upright piano and a platform with an American flag.

Two men sat on the platform, one in uniform with his
arms folded in front of his chest, the other in a suit, his
hands clasped around his crossed legs. A third man stood
at a microphone. He also wore the uniform. The microphone looked like a stick in his hand. "Welcome friends,"
he said. The words blasted out at the audience, trailed by

a thin, high, wailing sound. At one side of the platform, someone adjusted the volume on the loudspeaker equipment. The speaker tried again. "Welcome friends." In the small hall there was no need for a microphone at all.

Max took a seat in the last row. The hall was not more than half full, a largely middle aged crowd with a scattering of young men and lone old women an informal shirtsleeve crowd, though a few men wore suits. Max felt conspicuous in his best suit. Just down the aisle, a man took off his jacket and rolled up his sleeves and as the air in the hall warmed up and thickened Max knew he would be tempted to do the same. He could take his jacket off, but he could not roll up his sleeves without revealing the row of blue numbers on his forearm. Only the people in uniform looked stiff and ceremonious. There were some of them in the front row and three more standing against the back row. Now Max saw that some of the people who wore suits also wore swastika armbands. A fat man with a cannonball head who wore an armband was talking to the three uniformed youths in the back of the hall. Max turned sideways so he could watch them out of the corner of his eye until they stopped talking and Max realized they were watching him. He faced the speaker and sank down a little in his chair.

"It's the same old pattern," the speaker was saying. "Any set of trumped-up charges is good enough against a member of the National Resurgence Party. They don't dare try young Mort Holtz for his beliefs; no, they want to make him out a raper of young girls. Well, some of you know Mort Holtz." Max listened closely as the speaker described Holtz's boyhood in the orphanage and then how he had come to San Francisco where he met members of the Party. Max wondered where he was the day Holtz became a Nazi. Had they ever passed each other on the

106

Max took a deep breath and climbed the stairs.

street? Perhaps they had bumped into each other in a crowd and excused themselves like strangers.

"We are gathered here tonight because the National Resurgence Party does not abandon its members in time of need. Mort practically grew up in our Party. Now our Party will grow up around Mort Holtz."

Max suddenly realized that either way they could not lose. If Holtz were acquitted, the Party would be vindicated; if he were found guilty and executed, they would have a martyr.

A burst of applause sprang from the audience. Max clapped his hands twice, then once more. The speech was over. Max sneaked a glance at the back of the hall where the doorman had joined the fat man and the three uniformed youths.

A thin, nervous young man stepped to the microphone and a woman went to the piano. Clutching the microphone, the young man announced a popular song. The pianist began an introduction which the singer followed with his lips and at her signal he plunged in, but he was late and he never quite caught up. The next song they managed to do together, his glassy eyes fixed on the ceiling somewhere over the middle of the audience, her face close to the keyboard. Max wondered if it would be all right to go to the men's room if there was one, but just then the doorman tapped him on the shoulder and beckoned Max to follow him.

The three youths had taken seats in the hall, but the fat man still waited just outside the door. "What's your name?" the fat man asked.

"Max."

"What's your last name?" He did not sound threatening. Except for the armband he could have been an office clerk or a census taker.

"Warner," Max said, mentally recording another demerit. "Max Warner." When he was a boy his mother always knew when he lied because his face turned red. He prayed his face was not red now.

"We haven't noticed you around here before. Is this your first time?"

"Yes. It said in the paper everyone was invited."

"Certainly," the fat man said. "Everyone is invited."

Then the doorman stepped up closer and asked, "Are you Jewish?"

"Jewish?" Max gripped the sleeve of his jacket.

"Now, Paul," the fat man admonished his companion. But he turned and waited for Max to answer.

"Jewish? Would I be here if I were Jewish?"

"Well, we didn't really think so," the fat man said, adjusting his armband. "Interested in the Party?"

Max's mouth was too dry to make words. He nodded.

"Wait a minute." The fat man went to a room near the entrance to the hall and left Max and the doorman staring at each other. He came back a minute later with some pamphlets and a card on which he asked Max to write his name and address. Max took the card to a table by the door. He had to lean his wrist hard against the table in order to control the pencil as he made up an address. Then he took the pamphlets and went back inside the hall. The singer and the piano player were taking a bow. Max's hand was shaking and he could feel perspiration on his forehead, but he didn't dare wipe it off.

Max heard the door behind him open and close again. All over the hall heads began to turn, but Max stared straight ahead, relaxing only when one of the men on the platform jumped up to introduce the Western Division Commander of the Party and Max saw a tall man in uniform move slowly down the center aisle. People began to stand. At the back of the hall, the three uniformed youths, the doorman, and the fat man all stood at attention. Slowly, Max got to his feet, his head slouched forward. He closed his eyes and did not open them until he heard the sound of people taking their seats again and when he looked the Western Division Commander stood on the platform, his arms folded, his marble eyes fixed on the audience.

With apparent reluctance the Commander unfolded his arms and stepped to the microphone. He had an almost square face with a jaw that jutted out like an open drawer and a head shaved so that a turf of gray hair rose from it. He pulled the microphone up to his level and in a voice that exploded as if he had been saving it up for this moment, he immediately began talking about what he called the International Jew Communist Conspiracy. "Who runs the world?" he shouted. "Washington and Moscow! Jews and Communists! The little guy is out in the cold. But not when he belongs to the National Resurgence Party."

Max felt an old chill sweep his body. The Commander's words seemed to change from English to German and Max remembered the store front meeting halls in Berlin when in 1930 and '31 he would sometimes stop for a minute outside and listen to the speeches until someone came out, someone wearing a brown shirt and boots and a swastika armband, and push him away. His father told him to stay away from those meetings, but once, after Mordecai was killed, he stood outside a meeting hall itching to go in and tell them about his grandfather until a boy in the brown shirt uniform, younger than Max, came out and slapped him. Max could still feel the sting of the boy's hand.

The Commander was talking about Holtz: "A clean

110

cut young man who wanted nothing better than to serve his fellow men. The agents of the Jew Communists have framed him. They know he is innocent. Would he have been arrested if he didn't belong to our Party?" The audience shouted "No!" "Would he be in jail now if he belonged to the Democrat or Republican or Communist Party?" Some people in the audience rose to the chorus of "No!" The Commander stood on his toes to shout, "Mort Holtz is a hero!"

While the audience stood and applauded, Max remembered Horst Wessel, the young Nazi storm trooper killed in the Berlin street fighting in 1930 who left behind a song that became the unofficial anthem of the Nazis. Max saw that these people would make a martyr out of Holtz just as the Nazis did out of Horst Wessel. The Jews did not leave their houses the day of the funeral, but afterwards Max saw newsreels of it, the Germans lining the street, the old men at attention, the old women weeping. When they heard the funeral procession go by in Max's house, his mother spit. Now Max hoped that Holtz did not write songs.

The man in the suit who had sat quietly through the meeting was introduced as Holtz's lawyer. He took a bow and then the announcer asked for a collection. Holtz's defense, he said, would cost money. Men in armbands lined both sides of the audience and began passing baskets down the aisles. "This is a time for sacrifice," the announcer said. The plate came to Max half full of coins and a few one dollar bills. Max put another five dollar bill in the plate and the man who took the plate from him reached out to pat him on the shoulder.

When the collection was completed, dancing was announced. Everyone got up and began to fold the chairs and carry them to the sides of the hall. They all seemed to know exactly what to do except Max. He stood in front of his chair wondering if he should help when he saw that an old woman who had been sitting in the row in front was standing alongside him now and smiling pleasantly. Max excused himself and took his chair to the side of the hall. Then he left. He thought he heard someone call him as he hurried down the stairs, but he did not look back or wait.

Outside, the deep voice of a foghorn drifted in from the bay. Max ran downhill towards the lights of the city until he found a taxi. All the way home, the strains of the Horst Wessel Song pounded in his head.

14

One thing was clear: he could not allow Holtz to become a martyr. So it had to be the boy. The only question now was how to go about it. If he went to the police they would want to know why he waited all this time. A better course was writing an anonymous letter. Then he would have done his duty and he wouldn't be bothered by a lot of unpleasant questions. He went to the bureau and took out the girl's button and then at the table that served him for a desk he spread a piece of stationery. Now that he saw clearly that he had no other choice he felt liberated by his decision, and the idea of the anonymous letter was the perfect means by which to rid himself of the problem completely. He hummed to himself as he lifted his pen, but no words would come. After staring at the blank sheet of paper for a long while, he put down the pen and placed the button on top of the paper. There was time in the morning to write the letter.

He sat down to it again after breakfast, but it looked

like such a nice day out he decided instead to call Clara. He hurried downstairs and listened for the Thompsons. "Hello," he called. There was no answer and remembering that it was Sunday, he quickly leafed through the phone book so he could call before they returned from church. He was dialing the number when the door opened.

"Good morning, Mister Friedman," Mrs. Thompson said.

Max slammed the phone down.

"Bad news?" Mr. Thompson asked, indicating the phone.

"What?" Max said. "Oh, the phone. No, it's all right."

"It was a lovely service today," Mrs. Thompson said. She wore a white hat with a veil and white gloves which she was just peeling off. "It's a shame you couldn't have been there."

When Max first moved in, Mrs. Thompson tried to get him to go with them to church. Each Saturday afternoon she would say, "Shall we wake you tomorrow morning for church?" until he explained that he was Jewish. She seemed genuinely puzzled at that and though she did not ask him again, whenever they met on Sunday morning she was sure to tell him what a nice service he had missed.

Mr. Thompson, struggling out of his tie, said in a loud whisper: "You can take my place next Sunday if you want."

Mrs. Thompson turned red and marched into the kitchen.

"Thank you," Max said. He slid by Mr. Thompson in the narrow hallway and went out to call.

Just as he was about to hang up, Clara's voice floated out of the receiver. He quickly pressed it to his ear again. "Hello, please," he heard her say.

"Clara? Mrs. Axelrod? Did I wake you?"

113

"Who is this?" she asked, still panting for breath.

Disappointed, Max considered hanging up. For a moment there was only the sound of Clara's breathing on the line as if he had tuned in to the winds of some vacant world. "It's me," he said at last, "Max Friedman. From the Agency."

"Of course," she said, her voice rising from the low tone of propriety to one of warm familiarity. "Forgive me Max. I should have recognized ."

Max sighed with relief. "You're sure I didn't wake you? I can call back."

"Oh, no. I was just going downstairs when I heard the phone. How are you?"

They talked a little about the weather before Max asked if he could see her. "I was just going to the park," she said. "Would you like to join me?"

"That's fine," Max said without enthusiasm as the shadow of the boy leaping out of the bushes passed through his mind.

"I'll bring sandwiches, " Clara said.

He met her by the Tenth Street entrance and as they passed the path leading to the grove where the girl had been killed, he ached to tell her about Holtz and the boy, but he held his tongue and looked the other way and soon they were in the Music Concourse.

"Do you come to the concerts?" Clara asked.

"On Sundays it's usually too crowded for me," Max said, though there were not as many people there now as he expected.

"I don't like the band concerts too much. All that oom-pahpah," Clara said, "but I come sometimes when they have the different days. I like it on French Day and Irish Day and especially on Israeli Independence Day, the danc-ing is beautiful. Let's to go the Tea Garden."

Max suddenly realized that Clara was carrying the picnic basket. He lifted it gently from her arm, hoping she did not see him blush, as they passed through the carved wooden gate of the Japanese Tea Garden. Here the Sunday crowds squeezed into the narrow paths and Max squirmed as he found himself imprisoned in a large family outing while Clara walked a few steps ahead, pointing at the arched bridge where children scrambled up the steep steps. She was saying something he couldn't hear. After maneuvering in several directions, he broke free and caught up to her in time to hear her say, "There's so much peace here. I come almost every week."

"It's beautiful," Max said. They stood in line for the stepping stones across the brook and then made their way to the giant Buddha.

"Look at him," Clara said, "how peaceful he looks."

Max looked up at the placid, squatting figure. "What is he smiling at?" Max asked as a pigeon fluttered to the Buddha's head.

"He smiles at what's inside of him," Clara said.

Max thought a minute. "It's easy to smile if your insides are made of stone," he said.

"Max!"

They left the Tea Garden and found a meadow where they ate lunch. "I hope you like cold pot roast," she said, handing him a thick sandwich. "I love it," he told her, matching eyes with her for a moment before biting into the crisp roll. "Ach," he said, his mouth full. "Wonderful!" She smiled and spread the rest of the lunch out on the tablecloth.

For a while neither of them spoke and Max, to avoid her eyes, studied the trees at the edge of the meadow. In Berlin at this time the leaves were choking to death in red and yellow and orange, but here the trees went on being green.

"What are you thinking?" Clara asked.

"I was just wondering if the trees ever died here. All these years I lived in San Francisco and I can't remember whether or not they die. You can't even tell what season it is here."

"Sure you can," Clara told him. "In the summer it doesn't rain, so if it's raining you know it must be one of the other seasons."

Max stood up suddenly, straining for memory.

"What is it, Max?" Clara asked, alarmed.

"A poem by Rilke I was trying to remember. 'O Tree of life, how do you know when winter comes?' No, that's not it." He closed his eyes. "Something like that. In the *Elegies*." He sent his mind back once more, but it could not get through the barbed wire of his years. "Do you know Rilke?" he asked Clara, sitting down again and selecting a peach from the picnic basket.

"No," she said. "My favorite is Edna St. Vincent Millay."

"An American?"

Clara nodded.

"I don't know her. Actually, I only know Rilke from a course at the university. I don't care for modern poetry so much."

"The university, Max? What did you study?"

"Literature. I liked best of all Schiller. And of course Shakespeare."

He started to tell her about his university days and how he wanted to be a professor, but now memory did come back and arguments with Sarah echoed in his mind. "Then they kicked all the Jews out of the universities," he concluded.

"I didn't know that," she said. They finished eating in

116

silence and then Clara said, "My father was seventy- two years old when he started college."

"Is that so?" Max said. "Seventy- two? I guess it's never too late to start."

"Or to finish either," Clara said.

Max did not answer. When everything was gathered back into the wicker basket, they just got up and began to walk in no special direction until they came to the lake. For a while they watched the boats weave about on the sun capped water and then Max asked if she would like to go rowing. "Sure," she said. "Full steam ahead."

Max rented a boat, hoping he could still row. He held the boat for her as she climbed in. "Careful," he said. Then he climbed in, holding onto the sides to keep the boat from rocking. The attendant pushed the boat away from the dock and Max quickly put the oars in the locks, but he got them in backwards. "It's been a long time," he said, but he did not think yet of how long it had been. The boat drifted back to the dock where the attendant pushed it out again. Max righted the oars and began to row. At first it was easy, but before they reached the island in the middle of the lake, his arms began to ache and he let the boat drift a little. "Isn't this beautiful?" Clara said, gently rocking back and forth. "I would like some day to live on a houseboat. What do you think, Max?" But Max did not hear. He was remembering the last time he rowed. He and Sarah had gone all the way across town to the *Tegeler See* on a hot summer day. "Don't row so fast," Sarah had said, but Max rowed even faster and laughed along with Sarah who said, "Max, you're showing off," until he collided with a boat manned by two *Hitlerjugend*. A blondhaired boy at the oars, only a couple of years younger than Max, yelled: "I knew Jews were dumb, but I didn't know they were blind too," as he used his oar to separate the two

117

boats, and his young companion sitting in the stern said, "What can you expect from a Jewish sailor?" The boys laughed. Max yelled back, "If you don't watch out, I'll ram you again." The boats drifted apart. Just as Max bent to the oars, the younger boy made an obscene gesture and Max answered by shaking his fist at them. "My hero," Sarah said.

"Watch out!" Clara shouted. Max maneuvered the boat around in time to avoid grounding on the island.

Later, standing in front of Clara's house, the late afternoon wind embracing them and dark clouds sailing the sky, she asked him in to dinner. "I should ask you out to dinner," Max said gallantly. "Another time," Clara said. In front of her door she said, "I only have liver," and Max said, "I love liver."

Arnold was on the couch reading when they came in. He kissed his mother and shook hands with Max. When Clara went to the kitchen to start dinner, Max, who could think of nothing to say to the intense adolescent across the room said, "Go ahead and read. Don't let me interrupt." Watching him bent over his book, Max wondered if Arnold went out with girls. "What are you reading?" he asked. The boy looked up. "I'm studying French," he said. "For college."

"If you were studying German I might be able to help. Why are you taking French?"

"We had to take either French or German so I took French because I don't like Germany."

Max laughed and Arnold immediately turned back to his book. "I'm sorry," Max said. "I wasn't laughing at you."

The boy kept reading, whispering his French pronunciations.

"I mean it," Max said. "I was laughing at myself. We

used to do the same thing."

Arnold looked up. "What same thing?"

"Not speak German because we hated the people who spoke it. Even my wife used to say to me, 'Speak Yiddish,' and we all went around pretending we didn't understand German when it was really Germans we didn't understand."

Arnold stared at Max. "Who wants to understand them?"

"Everyone should, " Max said, speaking quickly now to keep up with his ideas. "If you understand them then you can't hate them."

"That's what I mean, " Arnold said, closing his book and standing up. "I want to hate them. Should we love them for what they did?"

Max could feel the door of his mind opening again, his thoughts sailing in the fresh breeze of argument. "Because I understand someone doesn't mean I have to love him. I can dislike him, I can even find him obnoxious. And I can certainly disagree with him. In fact, how can I disagree with someone I do not understand?"

"So then what do you do?"

"If I consider his ideas wrong then I can argue. If I think he is dangerous then I can even fight him. But if I hate him, then I can't win."

Arnold threw his arms in the air and slapped them against his side. "Why not?" he demanded.

"Because if I hate him I will not be content to beat him, I will want to destroy him. And if I succeed I will have committed a wrong as great or greater than any I could possibly oppose."

It was like the old days in the cafés. While Arnold thought about what Max said, Max remembered what it was like in the time when he was going to be a professor and he sat with his friends in the coffee houses and beer gardens arguing morality and politics, in the time when they were all going to be professors.

Arnold looked at him narrowly. "Did you understand the Germans?"

"No, I didn't. I only hated them and so I could not fight them. Knowing I could not destroy them, I pretended it was not my struggle, until in the end they almost destroyed me."

Arnold looked at his feet. After a minute he sat down and opened his book. "I'll probably have to take German in college anyway."

Max had been out to Berkeley a few times and walked around the campus. Yes, he thought, I will go back to the university. He wanted to ask Arnold about college, but the boy was studying again and Max did not want to interrupt. He looked around the room. How long does it take to cook liver, he wondered, but just then Clara called them in and there was vegetable soup too. It was thick and fragrant. "You made this just now?" Max asked.

"It's from a can, but I fixed it up a little," Clara said, urging everyone to eat.

Max had the feeling that Arnold was watching him out of the corner of his eye. He wondered what sort of impression he had made on him. "French he studies," Max said.

"What's wrong with French?" Clara asked.

"You can't read Schiller in French."

Arnold and his mother stared at each other while Max went on eating. "That's good," Max said, wiping the last drop of soup from his mouth. Perhaps, he thought, Arnold will say something about their conversation himself. But Arnold said nothing for the rest of the meal and afterwards he excused himself and went into his room to read.

"I wonder what your son thinks of me," Max said while he and Clara did the dishes.

"He's a little jealous," Clara said. "Maybe a little afraid too. He was very close to his father."

"So were you," Max said. He was immediately sorry he said it, but Clara did not let him apologize.

"How did your husband die, if I may ask?"

"A heart attack. Out there on the stairs. He wasn't sick a day and then just like that he was gone."

"I'm sorry," Max said. "I shouldn't have said anything. It's not my business."

"No, I'm glad you asked." Clara handed Max the last wet dish. When it was dry she went into the living room. Max followed. He knew she was going to say something that was difficult for her to say and he considered leaving and sparing her the embarrassment, but she began before he could say anything.

"You know," she said, "after you left the other night I was thinking what Jack, my husband, would think if I went out with another man. I wondered if it was like cheating on him. You understand. But Jack, may he rest in peace, was never a selfish man. He was always sorry we only had one child because he loved children and he used to say, 'You can't get too much of a good thing.' No, the man I loved wouldn't want me to be alone and unhappy, I'm convinced. I'm just telling so you'll understand, but if you don't want to come any more, then it will be my turn to understand. You don't have to say anything."

Max was glad he stayed. He went over to her chair and took her hands in his. "Clara," he said. And then all he could think of to say was, "Will you have dinner with me next week?"

"That would be very nice," she said. Tears formed in the corners of her eyes.

They talked until it was dark and then Clara said she was tired. Max said he would go. "Friday night?" he said.

She said that would be fine. "Perhaps we can go to the movies too," he said.

At a knock on the bedroom door, Arnold came out to say goodnight. Max held out his hand, but the boy only nodded and went back to his room so Max took Clara's hand instead and held it all the way to the door.

When he got home, Max saw the button lying on the sheet of stationery on the table and he sat down to write to the police. The words would still not come to him and instead of writing he tried to imagine what it would be like when the police received his anonymous letter. He saw policemen stopping boys on the street, Harold's picture in the post office. Suddenly he slapped himself on the head. *Dummkopf!* You're the only witness. How can you be anonymous? Of course, he thought, getting up and pacing about the room, what's the use of turning the boy in if I'm not willing to testify. And if I'm willing to testify what's the point of writing anonymous letters?

He seized the button and wrenched open the window and stood there, his arm raised like an athlete's, bending to it, urging his arm forward. But the button weighed a hundred pounds in his hand and his arm would not go forward. Finally, he put it back in the drawer with his socks. He wished he had never seen Golden Gate Park, but he remembered the afternoon there with Clara and his eyes filled with tears.

15

If he were going to turn the boy in, it were best done quickly, Max decided. The telephone seemed the proper instrument. He could call the police and tell them what he knew and then if they wanted him to come down, he would already have committed himself. But each time he approached a telephone he saw the boy down on his knees or felt still his thin hands clasping his arm and heard his unripe voice crying, *I don't want to die, I don't want to die*, until it was Friday and Holtz was back in the paper. A jury had been impaneled; his trial was about to begin. Reading the story, it occurred to Max that if Holtz were found innocent, there would be no need to turn the boy in. And having waited this long, it was certainly worth waiting another week. That decision made, Max turned to the entertainment section. The Actors' Workshop was doing *Coriolanus* and Max immediately called to make reservations. When he lived downtown he went to the theater two or three times, but he could never imagine himself seeing a play or a movie without Sarah next to him in the dark. Finally he stopped going, afraid he would grab the hand of the stranger next to him. Besides, he told himself, a play without someone to discuss it with afterwards was like a dinner without a dessert. There was no answer at the box office and hanging up the phone, Max wondered if Clara liked Shakespeare. Of course she does, he told himself.

He made the reservations during his lunch hour and then he spent the rest of the afternoon watching the clock. A few minutes before five he straightened his tie and brushed the lapels of his blue suit. "A girlfriend?" Shmuel asked, sniffing the air. Max pretended he didn't hear.

He took her to a French restaurant he had heard Dr. Resnick talk about. "It's too fancy," Clara said as Max urged her in, wishing he had taken her instead to the Jewish restaurant he was more familiar with, or the Russian restaurant out on Geary. Clara surrendered her coat to the girl in the checkroom and then they followed the headwaiter to a booth where they sank into plush leather seats and found themselves squinting through candlelight at long, unwieldy menus while another waiter appeared like a private secretary, pad and pencil poised as if for dictation.

"We should have brought Arnold to read the menu," Clara said, whispering so the waiter would not write it down.

"Arnold?" And then Max remembered that Arnold was studying French and he laughed softly. He described as many of the dishes as he could, remembering that the last time he had been in a French restaurant it was with Sarah in Berlin and the restaurant was owned by a German who had been captured at Verdun. Clara said she would like *coq au vin* and Max chose the *Saumon aux Herbes en Papiotte*. When the waiter asked what they would like to drink, Max ordered champagne, but Clara refused and they settled for a Burgundy suggested by the waiter.

They waited quietly for the food to come. Finally, Clara said, "I forgot to tell you, they called me for an interview at the public library. I applied months ago."

The waiter put the soup before them.

"Wonderful," Max said.

"The soup or the library?"

"Both. When is the interview?"

"Monday."

They talked about the library until the wine steward came and poured some wine into Max's glass and waited for him to taste it. Max took a sip. "Good," he said. "Good." The steward filled both their glasses.

"A toast," Max suggested, holding up his glass.

Clara touched her glass to his and looked around. "What shall we toast?"

"To- " What he wanted to say would not come out.

"To Shakespeare," he said instead.

124

After the waiter brought the entree Max said, "You know, Clara, I've been thinking about your father."

"My father?" Clara said, holding a forkful of green beans half way to her mouth.

"About him going to college when he was seventy-two. I was thinking maybe I could go back and finish."

"That's wonderful, Max." She put her fork down and leaned closer to him.

"Of course, I might have to start all over. I don't know. But I was wondering if it's too late for me to become a teacher."

"It isn't, Max. I know it isn't."

"You really think so? I'm going to look into it. Maybe I can start with a night course."

"You're wonderful, Max."

He bowed his head a little and then resumed eating. After a moment, he could hear Clara eating again too.

"Not bad," Max said later, as the busboy cleared the dishes away.

"Not bad?" Clara gasped. "To make chicken like that you have to be a genius."

"Then you're a genius," Max said. Even by candle-light he could see that she was blushing.

People were leaving on every side and the busboys worked faster, but the waiter did not come with their dessert. Max finished the wine and glanced at his watch. "Look what time it is. We'll be late for the play."

"We could skip the dessert," Clara suggested, but just then the waiter appeared wheeling the pastry cart and they decided to stay. Max ate an éclair in three bites and Clara nibbled steadily at a *petit four* until it was gone and soon they had a taxi and were in the theater, but the play had started.

"The poor people of Rome are rebelling because they

are hungry," Max explained. "Coriolanus, who is a famous soldier, comes along and tells them they don't deserve food because they are not brave."

All around Max people turned and shushed him with fingers to lips. "Quiet please," one man said loudly.

Max nodded to everyone. A moment later he turned to Clara again. "I forgot to tell you. He's not called Coriolanus yet. That comes later," and he joined everyone else in a chorus of "shh!" as if the audience had sprung a leak. He giggled softly when Clara looked at him, but he did not speak again during the play.

When he said goodbye that night she looked up at him and he kissed her. "I'll see you tomorrow," he said. It was not a question and she did not answer.

All day Saturday, he thought of Sarah. He woke up certain she was lying next to him and even when he tried to think about Clara, to recall her laugh, the touch of her hand and lips, it was Sarah's face that conjured in his mind. That evening, on his way to Clara's house, he remembered how he had courted Sarah. She was seventeen when he met her and her parents were very strict. For almost a year they would not let her go out with Max unless one of them went along so they spent many nights in her room whispering so that her parents would not overhear until one of them, usually her father, would knock on the door and ask what was going on in there. Sometimes, because there was a play or a movie they wanted to see, they consented to go with Sarah's mother, but they had a trick: they would go late when three seats together were hard to find and they usually managed to end up sitting together with Sarah's mother a row or two behind where, between films, she would lean over and whisper loudly, "Is everything all right?" Only Sunday afternoons were they allowed to go out alone, her parents evidently believing that you cannot make love on Sunday afternoon, but they were wrong. One Sunday a friend loaned them his apartment. It was the first time for each of them. The friend was not Jewish. Max met him at the university where Max was in his first year. He often wondered what happened to him. His name was Ernst and he smoked an imported brand of sweet smelling cigarettes and burned incense in his room. Max could always recall the smell of the incense. He smelled it later that night when he made love to Clara.

It was Clara who first mentioned marriage. Max came over Sunday morning with bagels and lox he had gone all the way downtown to get and after Arnold left to go hiking on Mt. Tamalpais with a club he belonged to, Clara said, "It would be terrible for a person never to know love."

"Yes," Max agreed.

"Or marriage," Clara added.

"Yes," he said, and then he changed the subject because he knew he was not through thinking about Sarah. They spent the day in the park and then for dinner Clara made chicken liver and potato kugel. "You ought to open a restaurant," Max said. "You would make a fortune." Later, they stood by the bedroom door, but they did not go in. Arnold came home tracking mud in the house and asking his mother if she would run the bath for him. Max talked to him about hiking until his bath was ready and then he kissed Clara goodnight and went home to reminisce about his life with Sarah.

She was eighteen and they were allowed at last to go out by themselves. They planned to marry as soon as Max graduated and started teaching, but a law was passed excluding all but a few Jews from the universities. For a while, Max was allowed to stay because his father had been in the army during the First World War. They gave him a special student card with a yellow stripe. Even after Sarah tore it up he kept attending, saying things would get better. When they discovered him without his card and expelled him from the university he said things were bound to change. He got a job writing advertising copy for an uncle who owned a department store. Sarah wanted to leave the country, but he pleaded with her to stay and marry him, and she did. Her parents were orthodox and they insisted on an orthodox wedding, including the traditional *mikvah*. For days they argued about whether to tell her favorite aunt that she was not a virgin. Sarah wanted to tell her, but Max said no. Sarah finally agreed, but Max was sure the old aunt winked at him after the ceremony. For months afterward he was afraid to speak to her.

Then the department store was taken away from his uncle and he was out of a job. For a while they both worked in the tailor shop. He remembered how he would look up at her and how the tears came to his eyes to see her bent over a suit or a dress, sewing away as if it were important to her. "*Sarah, mein Schatz*," he said once, but she told him to speak Yiddish.

The memories were painful. Max could feel the headache gathering force just behind his eye and he sat on the edge of the bed holding his head in his hands as he remembered, but he couldn't stop. It was like being forced to watch a movie. And the memory he could never forget, the sound of the boots on the steps and the heavy knock on the door. "Come along," one of the SS men said. And the thing he would like most to forget: going down-stairs he asked, "Where are we going?" and Sarah laughed at him.

The next morning, waiting for the bus, he was looking at the display of rings in a jewelry store, but he saw Sarah's reflection in the window. *Remember*, she said, and then the bus came.

Clara called him at work to say she got the job at the library. "That's wonderful," Max said, whispering into the telephone, his back turned to Shmuel. "I'll come over after work and we can celebrate."

"Bring some candy," Shmuel said.

"Big ears!" Max said, returning to his desk.

Shopping for candy after work, Max noticed something about Holtz in the evening paper and he began to sweat and tremble. A jury had been chosen, the trial would begin tomorrow. He called Clara to say he was not feeling well.

16

He was halfway to work when he knew he must attend the trial and, thinking he could transfer at the next street, he pulled the cord and stumbled down out of the bus only to stare for a moment in the direction of downtown and then at the houses around him. It was the wrong stop. The newspaper that recounted the crime with pictures of Holtz and the girl's body covered by the sheet in the little grove was unpeeling in his hands and he threw it away page by page and set off for the downtown bus two blocks away.

In the marble corridors of the Hall of Justice he called the agency to say he was not feeling well and then he asked the blind man at the newsstand where the Holtz trial was being held.

"Third floor and turn to your left," the blind man said, adding, "It must be quite a show."

Max jabbed at the elevator button. The doors slid open immediately and Max rushed gratefully in and out again a moment later on the third floor. In a corridor to his left were a row of courtrooms and Max went down the row, peering into the little windows in the doors until he came to one where people were standing, their backs blocking the window. Max stopped there, but he had never been in a courtroom before and he wondered if it was all right to go in during the trial. Finally he made up his mind and he opened the door slowly and squeezed in among the spectators at the back of the court. He could not see anything, but he held his breath and listened as somewhere in front a man was saying, "There is not one shred of real evidence to link my client to this case. Mortimer Holtz is being made a scapegoat, ladies and gentlemen of the jury, but after you have heard the evidence or lack of it I am sure you will have no part of it. Thank you."

"Who was that?" Max asked the man next to him.

"Andrew Tyler, the defense lawyer," the man said. "Those were was his opening remarks."

Some people were talking in the front of the courtroom, but Max could not make out what was being said. He pushed his way forward until he could see an American flag and a California flag flanking the judge's bench and then he could see the judge himself leaning back in his highback leather chair. The judge seemed to be thinking about something on the ceiling. Max followed his eyes to the banks of lights, but there was only the flickering of a bulb behind its thick glass panel. Max regarded the judge again. He kept the tips of his fingers together as if making a little play steeple and his face, framed by waves of white hair, concentrated on the flickering bulb, or, Max thought, perhaps on heaven itself so peaceful did the judge appear. Then, suddenly, he leaned down and spoke to someone Max could not see. "Call Doctor Anthony Capehart to the stand," a voice said, echoed by a louder voice that sang out: "Doctor Anthony Capehart."

Max squeezed between a fat woman carrying a shopping bag and a tall thin man in a suit who was cleaning his nails with a matchstick. "Stop shoving," someone behind him said and the fat woman gave him a terrible look as she hugged the shopping bag to her breasts, but Max paid no attention. He could see Doctor Capehart taking the oath and seating himself at the witness stand. Max could see the entire court now. In front of the witness stand, the court reporter sat, his fingers poised over his machine. Along the side sat the jurors. Max studied them carefully: eight women and four men sat in the jury box as they might sit in the bus at three o'clock. Max looked around for a familiar face, but recognized no one. Someone approached Dr. Capehart and began asking him questions.

"Who is that?" Max asked the tall man next to him.

He did not answer. Instead, the woman with the shopping bag said, "Gianetto. Gianetti."

"Gianelli," the tall man said, pronouncing each syllable as a separate word.

"The district attorney," the fat woman whispered.

"Assistant district attorney," the tall man said, looking straight ahead.

Max thanked them both.

It was established that Dr. Capehart was the county coroner. He testified that Linda Jordan had sex before she died and that death had occurred as a result of a severe cut on the neck resulting in the severing of the carotid artery. Mr. Gianelli paced lion like before the court, asking his questions as he made the turn in front of the witness. He was a short man who stooped over as he paced so that the judge occasionally leaned over to see what he was doing. Now he stalked the prosecutor's table and pounced on an object in a sack. He held it before the witness and revealed

131

the bottom two-thirds of a broken beer bottle. "Could this be the object that killed Linda Jordan?" he asked.

Dr. Capehart looked at the jagged edges of the bottle. "It could be," he said.

Gianelli thanked the doctor.

Tyler stood up and began his cross-examination. He did not pace like Gianelli but stood in front of the witness, blocking the audience from seeing.

"Was Linda Jordan raped, Dr. Capehart?"

"The appearance of her body was consistent with rape. There was a struggle and there was semen in her—"

"Come, come, Dr. Capehart. Was she raped or not?"

"I would say probably."

"Probably? But you can't say for sure?"

"No."

"She might have had sex some time before she died?"

"It's possible."

"That's all, Dr. Capehart." Tyler dismissed him as if he just failed an audition.

The next witness was a lab technician who testified that blood found on the bottle was the same type as Linda Jordan's and that a hair attached to it matched Linda Jordan's hair. The bottle was marked Exhibit A and Gianelli then asked permission to pass it among the jurors, bringing Tyler to his feet again.

"This is outrageous," he shouted.

"I take it, Mr. Tyler, that you object," the judge asked.

Tyler said that passing the bottle around would constitute a vulgar piece of exhibitionism and the judge agreed and sustained the objection, but Gianelli, holding the bottle piece up like a trophy, walked slowly past the jury box. In the courtroom the spectators leaned forward, and Max saw clearly the fragment of brown bottle that ended in what looked like rotting teeth. Gianelli handed it to a clerk to be marked for identification and the court relaxed, but Max saw the prosecutor smile to his assistant at the long table.

Max realized that Holtz must be at the other table. While a new witness was being called, he examined the row of heads. One he recognized as Tyler, leaning over the table and writing. There were two more men at the table; they were both young and wore suits, one in dark blue, the other in gray, and from the back either one could be Holtz. While a policeman was being sworn in, Max asked his tall neighbor which man was Holtz.

"In the blue suit," the man said, spitting the words out like pits from the corner of his mouth. "The table on the right."

"He won't wear a suit when they hang him," the fat woman to Max's left whispered.

Max thanked the thin man and started to explain to the fat woman that in California convicts were executed by gas, but he thought better of it. On the stand Gianelli produced the bottle again and the officer testified that he found it in the same grove where Linda Jordan died. But Max was hardly conscious of this testimony; he was staring at Holtz. He let his hair grow, Max observed, explaining why he had not picked Holtz out immediately. Turn around, Max thought, trying to send a telepathic message to Holtz. Turn around, he urged, anxious to see the face of the man who had brought him to the Hall of Justice when he should be working. "Turn around, troublemaker," he whispered. But Holtz did not move.

When Gianelli finished questioning the policeman, Tyler dismissed the officer without any questions and the judge declared a ten minute recess. About half the audience filed out and as they did so, Max pushed to the front and took a seat directly behind Holtz. His lawyer was conferring with the third man at the desk. Holtz sat perfectly still as if waiting to be wound up. "Holtz," Max whispered, leaning over the railing and then sitting back quickly as Holtz turned around.

"Did you call me?" Holtz asked.

Max shook his head and after looking over the rest of the audience, Holtz turned back, but Max had seen the face of the newspaper stories, the round face with the dark hair and the moustache and the pushed in eyes of a child's mistreated doll, familiar and repellant, like the face of an unnatural brother seen for the first time. Max stared at the neatly trimmed, flat head and Holtz's long, graceful neck. He felt like crying.

When he looked up, people were crowding into the row. "That's my seat," a man said. Max slid over against an old man wearing a hearing aid. Several people complained, but the judge was rapping his gavel and they sat squeezed into the row. The old man gave him a dirty look and the man on the other side shoved his elbow into Max's rib as the assistant district attorney called for Mister Arthur Jordan to take the stand and the quiet courtroom grew more quiet still. The clerk called the witness's name and the murdered girl's father took long strides down the aisle and through the swinging gate that separated the spectators from the participants, stopped and looked embarrassed at the audience, and then followed the clerk to the witness stand where he was sworn in. He was a large man and he stretched the suit he was wearing as if it weren't his. Gianelli leaped to his feet and began his pacing. "Are you acquainted with the defendant, Mortimer Holtz?" he asked, passing in front of the witness box. Even sitting in the witness box Jordan looked as if he would swallow the microphone.

"Yes," he said, looking not at Holtz but straight ahead,

at no one or, perhaps, at anyone who was not Holtz.

The court reporter pecked silently away at his machine.

"When was the last time you saw the defendant?" Gianelli emphasized the last syllable, spitting the word out.

"About a week before...." He finished the sentence, but no one heard it.

"Speak a little louder," the judge said.

The big man seemed to gather himself together, filling the box even more. "A week before Linda was murdered," he said, too loudly this time.

"Tell us in your own words what happened on that occasion."

Jordan fidgeted and then adjusted the microphone. "Holtz came to take Linda out. I think they were going to a dance or something. Well, I had argued with Holtz before about Hitler and when he came to the door I called Linda and I said, 'Your little stormtrooper is here.' And Holtz, he said 'When the New Order comes you will be taken care of along with the Jews.'"

"Objection," Tyler shouted.

Gianelli explained that he was going to show that Holtz had a motive for murdering Linda Jordan and the judge allowed the girl's father to proceed. The spectators all leaned forward and Max escaped the elbows of the man next to him.

"So I threw him out of the house," Jordan said, running his hand through his hair.

There was a long pause. Gianelli nodded. "Go on," he said softly. Jordan hunched his shoulders and raised his hands as if to speak by gesturing, but then he relaxed suddenly and said, "Linda ran out of the house after him. I waited up for her and when she came home I told her she was not to see Holtz again. We argued for a while, then she agreed that the following week she would tell him she wasn't allowed to go out with him anymore. She was always a good girl I-" Tyler got to his feet, but he sat down again without saying anything and Jordan continued: "-wanted her to call him or write to him, but I finally agreed to let her tell him. She thought it was the fair thing to do."

"Did you see Holtz that night?" Gianelli asked.

"No. She went out again and met him someplace, I don't know where. They arranged it over the telephone. She just went out and we never saw her again."

Gianelli faced the jurors; he looked as if he would take a bow. Behind Max a woman wept and several people turned around, but Max kept staring straight ahead.

"Your witness," Gianelli said. Tyler approached the witness, got close enough to touch him and then backed up and leaned against the juror's box. "To your knowledge, Mr. Jordan, did the defendant ever make a threat of any kind against your daughter?"

Jordan shook his head and the judge asked him to speak up. "No," Jordan said.

"Very good," Tyler said, looking significantly at the jurors. "Now tell us if you will, where did your daughter first meet my client?"

"I think it was at a dance."

"And how often did Linda and my client go out together?"

The girl's father adjusted his chair, leaving himself a little farther back in the witness box. "Four or five times," he said. "I would say five times."

"And did your daughter ever have sexual relations with my client?"

There was a gasp from the audience, which the judge

136

punctuated with his gavel even before Gianelli could shout "Objection!"

Tyler went before the judge. "Your honor, I just want to show the court that my client did not have any motive for raping the girl."

Gianelli almost pushed the defense attorney aside. "It would prove no such thing, your honor. The testimony is immaterial."

The judge contemplated the blinking light and rapped the gavel soundlessly against his palm. "I'll overrule the objection," he said. "You may answer the question, Mr. Jordan."

Jordan looked at Gianelli, but the prosecuting attorney waved his hand in the air and Jordan swallowed and said, "She may have. I don't know."

"You mean, don't you," Tyler stood before the witness box now, obscuring the witness from the spectators, "that she had relations with so many boys there's no doubt she had them with my client also?"

"Pig!" the old man next to Max said while comment crackled like electricity in the audience and the judge hammered the noise down.

Max touched the old man's arm. "It's important," Max told him. "He has to bring these things out." But the old man pulled his arm free and did not look at Max.

"Isn't it true," Tyler shouted while the audience buzzed and the judge hammered, "that your seventeen-year-old daughter owned a diaphragm?"

And now Gianelli could be heard above the audience shouting his objection. When the judge got the audience quiet he turned to Tyler and said, "Now that's enough, Mr. Tyler. You asked the question I allowed you to ask and the witness said he didn't know. Unless you can demonstrate the relevance of this line of questioning I will not let you

137

proceed with it any further." But Tyler was already walking back to the defense table.

On redirect examination Gianelli asked the girl's father if he feared for the girl's life when she was out with Holtz, but Tyler objected. Gianelli tried again. "Did Holtz seem to you a person capable of violence?" But Tyler objected that this called for the witness's opinion and the objection was sustained. Once more Gianelli paced and stopped before the girl's father. "He did say, didn't he, 'When the New Order comes you will be taken care of along with the Jews?' He said that to you?"

Mr. Jordan nodded. "Yes, he said that." And then he was allowed to step down.

Gianelli conferred with the judge and the spectators took the opportunity to talk to each other about the trial. Max tried to talk to the old man next to him. "Holtz didn't need to rape her, that's what the lawyer was trying to bring out. Don't you see what that means?" But the old man stared straight ahead and did not answer.

Tyler joined Gianelli before the judge and then all three looked at the clock and when they broke up, Gianelli called a Mr. Wishniak to the stand. The judge had to gavel for silence. Mr. Wishniak was a high school teacher who lived near Golden Gate Park. He testified that he had seen Holtz in the park on the night of the murder. "Where in the park?" Gianelli asked. "Near the grove where the girl was murdered," the teacher replied and people in the audience nodded as if this clinched the case. Gianelli rubbed his hands together as he turned the witness over to Tyler.

"Did you know the defendant?" Tyler asked.

"No, sir, I did not," Wishniak said.

"How did you know who it was?"

"I recognized his picture in the newspaper when he was arrested and I went to the police."

Tyler made him admit that it was dark in the park and that he did not carry a flashlight or speak to Holtz or even get a very prolonged look at him, but he could not shake Wishniak's identification and he finally threw his hands in the air and released the witness.

"Mr. Gianelli?" the judge said.

The prosecutor stood up, smiled at the jurors and announced that the prosecution rested. As the judge rapped his gavel, the back doors flew open and people started to leave. "Adjourn until nine o'clock tomorrow morning," the judge said, and the lawyers and their assistants and everyone else in the court began to pack their things and hurry out as if deserting a picnic threatened by rain.

Trapped in the front row, Max watched the bailiff lead Holtz out through a little door behind the judge's bench. When everyone was gone except Max and the old man, the old man pushing against him, trying to leave too, Max said, "The girl was a whore!" But the old man opened his jacket and turned off his hearing aid and then Max let him go.

That night Max went downstairs to watch the news on television. Mrs. Thompson sat in the easy chair, one hand resting on the china cat; the old man sat closer to the set and talked to the announcer.

"May I come in?" Max asked.

"Of course," Mrs. Thompson said. "Look who's here!" she told her husband. She had to repeat it, but then the old man turned around and welcomed Max. "Been keeping yourself busy lately?" the old man asked.

Max wondered what he meant, but the news was starting and he answered "Yes," and took a seat.

When the commentator described the first day of the trial a picture of Holtz was shown on the screen. "He's guilty,"

Mrs. Thompson announced. "You can see it in his eyes."

Max wanted to tell her it was an old picture, he could tell by the crewcut, but Mr. Thompson said, "I hope he gets what's coming to him," and then the commentator was talking about something else so Max didn't say anything at all. He hoped the jurors would not look too closely at Holtz's eyes.

In the morning, Max went down to the Hall of Justice early, but there were still several people ahead of him waiting for the courtroom to be opened. It was not until he was seated, again behind where Holtz would sit, and the courtroom was filling up that he remembered this too was a working day and he had not called to say he was still sick. He looked at the people filing in the door and decided not to risk losing his seat.

The jurors took their places. The lawyers assembled and then Holtz himself was led in. When the bailiff stood to address the court, everyone leaned forward, poised, ready. He asked the court to rise and with one sound they stood while the judge entered and waved them to their seats.

This was Tyler's day. The tall defense attorney wore a dark blue suit with a white handkerchief like a miniature sail showing from his breast pocket and a diamond stickpin in his tie that sometimes caught the light and sparkled like a star. He stood and waited for absolute silence. "Call Albert Foster," he said, but after the ringing way he called the witness, and after the way Foster strutted to the witness stand, the testimony seemed an anticlimax. Foster was a merchant seaman who kept a room in the same boardinghouse where Holtz lived. He considered himself and Holtz to be good friends. "Tell the jurors," Tyler pleaded, "what kind of person Mortimer Holtz really is. What was his reputation with his neighbors in the boarding house?"

It was Foster's opinion that Holtz would not hurt a fly. When Gianelli cross-examined him and asked about Holtz's Nazi philosophy, Foster said, "He doesn't really believe that stuff," but everyone saw Tyler push Holtz back into his seat and tell him to shut up.

Gianelli sat down and Tyler rose to ask the witness one more question. "Did you ever," he asked slowly, his back turned to the jury, "See Linda Jordan go to Mortimer Holtz's room?"

"Yes," Foster said. "Several times."

The witness was allowed to step down after that and Tyler stood before the court, scratching his chin as if contemplating his next move. Earlier, waiting for the trial to resume, the main topic of conversation among the spectators had been whether or not Holtz would be called to testify in his own behalf. Now, sensing that the time had come, the crowd leaned forward and began to whisper.

The judge leaned forward too and cleared his throat. "Mr.Tyler," he said. "Call your next witness."

Tyler looked out at the audience. "Mortimer Holtz to the stand," he said in his best Roman orator tone. Someone in the audience applauded foolishly and alone, the brief flurry of claps dying quickly like the salvo of a firing squad. The judge lifted the gavel and the bailiff stood ready to charge the audience, but neither was needed. A loud whisper penetrated the court: "I wasn't trying to be funny!"

When Holtz was sworn in and seated he stared straight ahead. In the first row, Max squirmed. Holtz's pushed in eyes seemed to Max to have picked him out, but Holtz's clay face remained blank. Max forced himself to look away. He followed Tyler who had stepped back to the defense table to consult some papers and who now approached the witness.

The first questions had to do with identifying himself and Holtz described his childhood, a lonely boy whose father deserted the family before Holtz was old enough to learn his name.

"And do you know his name now?" Tyler asked.

"No, sir," Holtz answered in his thin high voice that seemed to have gotten stuck in adolescence. "I never asked. I didn't want to know."

When Tyler nodded Holtz went on to tell about his mother, a woman who was good to him and taught him right from wrong, killed in an auto accident three years ago in Bixby, Arizona.

"And that's when you came to San Francisco?"

"Yes, sir. There were no jobs in Bixby."

He never looked at his lawyer; he didn't even address his answers to the jurors as some witnesses had done or to the judge as the girl's father sometimes did. Max turned around and tried to make out the line of Holtz's vision. There were only the leather paneled doors and the clock high on the back wall.

Now Tyler was asking Holtz if his political beliefs could ever lead him to the crime of which he was accused. "Oh no, sir. My beliefs have to do with society. They have nothing to do with this."

"If you please," his lawyer said, "would you describe for the ladies and gentlemen of the jury the events of the evening on which the crime took place."

"If you wish," Holtz said. Now he did acknowledge the jury, nodding to them as if they had just been introduced and then facing front again. "I met Linda around eight o'clock and we went to my place. She told me that her father had forbidden her to see me again. I said 'But you're seeing me now,' and she said it was for the last

142

time. Then she left alone."

"And did you and Linda have sex before she left?"

Holtz's face cracked. "Yes, sir," he said.

"What happened after she left?"

"Well, I just walked around for a while, wondering if I done the right thing by letting her go."

"What time was this?"

"I would say it was about nine o'clock."

Max looked back at the clock, thinking for a moment that Holtz was reading the time on the courtroom clock, but the time there was ten thirty.

"Is it possible you walked through Golden Gate Park?" Tyler asked.

"Yes, I did walk through the park. Definitely. But I did not murder Linda Jordan."

Tyler looked from his witness to the judge to the reporters to the jury and then back to Holtz. "One more question, Mr. Holtz." Tyler clasped his hands behind his back and started moving, retreating towards the defense table. "You testified that you did not murder Linda Jordan, but you did have sex with her. Did you rape her?"

"No," Holtz said, turning to face the jury. "She always gave me what I wanted."

Max slapped himself on the cheek, but the sound was lost in the larger sound of the general intaking of air, a mass inhalation that should have left a vacuum, that seemed for a moment as if it did leave a vacuum because all around people were coughing and the judge's gavel did not carry. Holtz stood up and began to move out of the witness box, staggering into the sound, the vacuum, but Gianelli was there, shoving him back into the witness chair and then the court seemed to fill with air again. The gavel was heard, and everyone could breathe.

Gianelli and Holtz stared at each other. "Isn't it true,"

Gianelli demanded, stabbing Holtz with his finger, "that you did not want to break off seeing Linda Jordan?"

Holtz's eyes rolled up, abandoning the contest with the prosecutor, to fix on their old target. He answered Gianelli very slowly, not choosing his words so much as explaining to a child. "It was strictly her father's idea."

"You had an argument about it?"

"We had a discussion about it."

"Why would a girl who was not going to see you any more have sex with you?"

"Ask her."

The gasp came from the spectators again and Gianelli leaned into it as he returned to his table, spitting out the words, "No more questions."

The judge looked over at Tyler who seemed to be studying the grain of the wood in the defense table. "Mr. Tyler?"

Tyler half stood. "The defense rests," he said.

The judge declared a recess for lunch and in the afternoon the attorneys addressed the jury. Max hurried back from lunch to take his seat in the first row and, long before the trial was to resume, the seats were filled and spectators lined the rear of the courtroom. Gianelli reviewed the case for the jurors, pointing out that Holtz had a motive for the crime because Linda Jordan was not going to see him any more and he could not account for his whereabouts when the crime was committed. Then he spoke about Holtz's philosophy. "He says that his Nazi philosophy has nothing to do with this case, that it only concerns society, but we remember that the people who shared his philosophy murdered six million people in cold blood." Then the prosecutor turned his back on the jury and started to walk away. People began to stir, believing he was finished, but he suddenly turned around and marched back to the jury box. "Is

144

it so hard to believe," he asked, "that a Nazi would murder an innocent person? Remember, you need only be satisfied of this man's guilt beyond a reasonable doubt. I am satisfied. I'm sure you are too. I ask you as mothers and fathers to bring back the only verdict possible in this case: guilty!"

The judge gaveled down the cries that swept the courtroom and Max, who found himself nodding at what the prosecutor said, wiped his brow and whispered to himself: *Guilty! The hell with him.* He wanted to get up and leave the courtroom now that his mind was made up, but Tyler was standing before the jurors, his head bowed a little. "Ladies and Gentlemen of the jury," he said, "I won't keep you long. I just want to remind you that in America a man is entitled to any philosophy he wants, even if no one else agrees with it. It doesn't matter that you don't like the defendant's views. I don't like them either. It only matters that his life is in your hands." He dug at the floor with his shoe and then he argued that the evidence in the case was not conclusive. "The prosecution has failed miserably to prove its case. Where are the witnesses? Where are the fingerprints? Remember, if there is reasonable doubt in your minds, you cannot convict, and there must be reasonable doubt because the prosecution's case is built entirely on hearsay and innuendo." He backed away from the jury box, but everyone seemed to know he was not finished. He paced back and forth and then stood again before the jurors, his hands outstretched. "If you send this innocent boy to the gas chamber," he said, "you will have it on your conscience the rest of your lives." For a moment the room was dead, and then Tyler thanked the jurors and sat down.

Now everyone turned to look at the clock. After some discussion in front of the bench, the judge declared a recess and he and the lawyers retreated to his study. The spectators began to file out, but Max sat where he was, wishing he had left earlier when, for a moment, he forgot what he knew. He should have told him, Max thought, addressing the empty rows, that we are not Nazis.

When court reconvened an hour later, the judge read his instructions to the jury and then they filed out. For a while the spectators stayed where they were, but after an hour they began to leave. "What's taking them so long?" a man asked Max.

Riding home on the bus that evening- word had gone around the spectators waiting in the corridor that the jurors had been locked up for the night and Max left the Hall of Justice picturing the twelve jurors locked in a cell, debating the case far into the night -Max found a seat facing sideways and tried to imagine himself one of the jurors. He went over the whole case again, saw Gianelli pacing back and forth like a lion, Tyler leaping up to object. *That's all the evidence?* Max asked his fellow jurors. *Well, we can't convict him on that.* The juror sitting next to him rattled his newspaper. *The boy's life is at stake*, Max said. *After all, ladies and gentlemen, we are not murderers.*

He was convinced Holtz would be acquitted and that night he called Clara and made a date for Friday night. He was so sure Holtz would go free that he decided to go back to work the next day, but later, watching television ("I hope they hang him," Mrs. Thompson cried when the announcer said the case had gone to the jury), he changed his mind and the next morning he was back at the Hall of Justice.

It was a gray morning. Fog drew a shroud over the city and Max shuddered as he went back into the marblelined lobby. Outside the courtroom a crowd was already waiting, smoking cigarettes and talking. At one end of the corridor he recognized some people from the rally at Wagner

Hall. They stood apart and looked very serious. Max stayed away from them. Near him a woman was saying that if the jury was out a long time that meant they would acquit him. Max moved on to the next group. Here a man said the longer they were out the more likely they were to find him guilty. Max wondered who these people were, what their interest in the case was. Some people were laughing and Max moved near to them, trying to find out what there was to laugh about when suddenly motion swept through the crowd. They were piling into the court-room. Max heard nothing, but he followed the crowd in and saw that the jury was in its place. The seats were all filled and Max had to stand. The judge waited until the room was quiet, then he asked, "Has the jury reached a verdict?"

A man stood up in the jury box. "Yes, your honor." *Everything will be all right*, Max told himself. *Everything will be all right.* The man in the jury box, a tall thin man who hunched dangerously over the railing, took a paper out of his pocket and read from it. Max tried to read his face. *Everything is all right*, his face seemed to say.

"We, the undersigned members of the jury, having heard all the evidence in the case and being convinced beyond a reasonable doubt, find the defendant guilty...." His last words were lost in the swelling noise of the court-room. "Guilty," people were saying. "He's guilty!" Max pushed forward. "NO!" he shouted, but no one in the cheering courtroom heard him.

17

After dinner there was a knock on the door. Max finished putting the dishes in the sink. "Just a minute Mrs. Thompson," he called, drying his hands. But it wasn't Mrs. Thompson at all. Max opened the door on Shmuel holding a bunch of roses wrapped in green paper.

"Shmuel, it's you?" Max asked.

Shmuel was either blushing or reflecting the color of the flowers. "How do you feel?" he asked softly, as if he were in a hospital. He tried a smile, changed it for a look of great seriousness, then smiled again.

"What are you doing here?"

"You were sick, I came to see how you were." But now Shmuel began to look from Max, dressed in his suit, to the bed. He sniffed the air. Max followed his gaze and suddenly remembering he was supposed to be sick, sagged a little and tried to look pale.

"I feel a lot better," Max said, and he invited Shmuel in.

Shmuel took the straight-back chair this time, leaving Max the easy chair. "How are things at the office?" Max asked.

"All right. A little busy maybe."

"I'm sorry you have to do my work."

"Don't be sorry. I enjoy it," Shmuel said. He waved the flowers as he spoke and some petals fell off. "Here," he said. "You got some water?"

Max took the bouquet and sniffed their perfume. "Why did you bring flowers?"

"What should I have brought, chicken soup?"

Max went to find something to put the flowers in. The only thing that would hold them was a glass and he had to place it so the flowers would lean against the wall. "They're very nice, Shmuel. Thank you."

Shmuel tapped his fingers on his thigh and sang a wordless song.

"Dr. Resnick sent you?" Max asked.

Shmuel stopped singing. "Why should Resnick send me? I just came to see how you were." He sounded hurt and he got up to leave.

"Stay, Shmuel, stay," Max said, getting up and pushing Shmuel back into the seat. He was glad for someone to talk to, even if it was Shmuel. "It was just a bad cold," he said, trying to remember if that was what he told the secretary when he called. "I'll be back to work tomorrow."

Shmuel sang a little more. Then: "I see your Nazi was found guilty," he said.

"What do you mean—*my* Nazi?" Max asked, starting up from his chair. He balanced awkwardly for a moment, and then completed the motion, rising and going to the kitchen so he could talk about the trial with his back to Shmuel, because just at the mention of it he felt the sweat squeeze out of his forehead. "Who's my Nazi?"

"That fellow in the park. That murdered that little girl. I remember you were interested in it because it happened near here. I guess you didn't see the paper today."

"She wasn't a little girl," Max said. "You want tea?"

"Thank you, " Shmuel said. "A cup of tea would be nice. I thought she was a little girl. Anyway the jury found him guilty today. He'll get what he deserves."

"I hope so," Max said. He put the water on to boil and hunted in the cupboard for tea bags. "Why did you call him my Nazi?"

"A joke. Because you were always asking about him."

"Some joke!" Max hung a tea bag in one of the cups, spooned instant coffee into the other, and then spilled the coffee back into the jar and put a teabag in the cup instead. "You think he deserves to die?"

"I wasn't on the jury," Shmuel said.

No, Max thought, *you weren't on the jury. But I am!* The water whistled and he made the two cups of tea. "Lemon?" he asked. He cut two slices of lemon and delivered the tea to Shmuel who nested in the big chair, his feet drawn up and his leather face relaxed so that the wrinkles were just cracks, singing, a Talmudic student taking a break for tea. "Tell me, Shmuel. Why did you come tonight?"

"To see how you were."

"I know. I mean, why do you care how I am?"

Shmuel sipped the tea. "Who else do I have to care about?" He said it so quietly that Max had to lean forward to hear. "Max," Shmuel said. "Be my friend."

Max took the rest of the tea in one swallow and got up to pace about the room. "What do you want me to do?" he asked.

Shmuel looked up, his face blossoming. "Teach me to play chess," he said.

Max looked at Shmuel as if he were crazy, but the question raised echoes of a small boy nagging his father: *Bitte zeige mir Schach zu spielen, Papa.* And Max's father would pull his arm away from the boy's grasp and go on playing, never taking his eyes from the board. It was always father's friend who said *Spaterhin,* later. One day Max found Grandfather Mordecai at the chess set. "But you don't play chess," the boy said, and Grandfather Mordecai said, "How can I teach you if I don't learn?"

Shmuel stood up. "Good night," he said, starting for the door.

"Wait," Max said. He took the chess set out of the

150

closet and blew the dust off. "One game," he said.

Max played very slowly, explaining his moves to Shmuel, and in the end they played another game and Shmuel was catching on, though Max still beat him easily.

"Thank you," Shmuel said, getting up from the table.

Max watched him put his coat on. "Shmuel," he said. Shmuel turned around. "If you were sick, I wouldn't come visit you."

Shmuel shrugged his shoulders, but whether to indicate that he understood or whether he was just adjusting his coat, Max didn't know.

"You hear, Shmuel?"

"Good night, Max. Thanks for the chess."

Max watched Shmuel go out, then he ran to the door. "Thanks for the flowers," he called. Shmuel, halfway down the steps, turned, but said nothing.

It was too late to watch the news on television so he went to sleep early instead. He was tired and he thought he would sleep well, but he kept waking up to voices that whispered *guilty*. He would look at the black window and yearn for morning, but when morning came only a rising tide of nausea made him get out of bed. He threw up in the toilet and then he flushed it and sat down at the kitchen table and watched his hands tremble. Sunlight kissed the window and over the roof of the house across the street a clear blue sky stretched all the way to heaven. He had dreamed that he was dressed in a brown uniform and boots and he had gone to someone's apartment. In the dream he knocked on the door with his fist and when the door opened it was Holtz pleading with Max not to take him away, but Max led him to a gray stone building with iron doors. Next to the building at a sidewalk cafe, Shmuel sat playing chess and inside the building voices chanted

151

guilty, guilty. Max went to the window: there was not even a fog to blame for his headache.

Every morning for the past three days he had called the agency to say he was not feeling well; now with his head throbbing and his stomach doing a waltz, he had to go to work. For a while he considered calling and saying he was sick again, but he looked at the flowers that Shmuel brought and he knew he could not call. The chess set was still set up on the kitchen table. Max saw at a glance that the game was not over. Shmuel's last pawn could interpose *en passant* and capture Max's knight in the process. The checkmate was not a checkmate and looking at the board, Max wondered how he could have failed to see it. He blamed it on not having played for so long and he wondered if he would have to apologize to Shmuel. The wooden figures seemed to mock him. Maneuvering Shmuel's pieces, he saw that he was closer to being checkmated than Shmuel was.

He made some coffee and drank it before it cooled, burning his tongue, but it made him feel better and he got dressed and hurried for the bus, his head still humming.

The familiar furniture of the office comforted him. He was a little late and some people were already waiting on the leather chairs in the reception room. Max nodded to the receptionist and did not even wait for her to ask him how he felt. He couldn't wait to get back to his desk.

"How do you feel?" Shmuel asked, looking up from a letter.

"Fine." He wanted to get to work, to read and file and sort and lose himself in other people's problems. "Oh, Shmuel," he said. "Thank you for the flowers." Shmuel kept reading and Max drummed his fingers on the desk and waited for the mail.

Finally Shmuel brought the mail over, spreading one

letter out before Max. "This is Mrs. Kipnis," he said. "She is in New Zealand and wants to know can we find a Jewish husband for her."

"You're not supposed to read the mail," Max told him. "Just open it."

"That's some job," Shmuel said, going back to his own desk.

Max watched his small back as it retreated. "I didn't mean it," he said. "Read the mail, Shmuel. What does it hurt?"

He began to line up his folders but he saw that Shmuel was still watching him from the middle of the room. *What does he want?* Max wondered. Then Shmuel went to his desk and Max started to work, but not in earnest yet because he knew that Doctor Resnick would be in soon to ask how he felt. He bided his time, arranging the folders on his desk until the door to the consultation room opened. Before the psychiatrist could say anything, Max said, "I feel much better. It was only a little cold. A bad cold." The psychiatrist nodded. "It's good to see you back," he said, and then he stood and watched like Shmuel had done and Max, sorting out the folders for the third time, cursed him under his breath.

At lunch time, Shmuel held up a chess set. "Not today," Max said, hurrying out to the luncheonette. He ate quickly and then walked three times around the block trying not to think of the boy and Holtz and the trial. Before the hour was up he was back at his desk, addressing envelopes and suffering Shmuel's questioning stare.

He preferred the letters that simply asked for information. To these people he could send a printed statement. Completed applications were a little more difficult. For each of these he had to see if the application was properly completed and if it was assign it to one of the consulting psychiatrists. The hardest letters to deal with were those that stated their problem either on an application Max had sent or in the letter itself. He had to decide whether to send an application or a form letter explaining that the agency could not be of help. Often, doing this, he thought of Clara. If she had written instead of coming to make a scene in the outer office, their relationship would have been limited to the form letter. Since meeting Clara he often wondered about the people he wrote to, but not today. With his mind poised on the edge of a cliff, two strategies seemed to lead to safety: working as fast as he could, and making the mail last all day.

At four o'clock the mail seemed to be holding out, but Max was slowing down. "Shmuel," he called. "Should I send an application to a woman who wants advice on getting an abortion?"

Shmuel's head jerked up. "You're asking me?"

"Sure I'm asking you. Is that a family problem or not?"

Shmuel closed his eyes to think. "Is she married?"

"She doesn't say."

"Ask her if she's married," Shmuel advised. Max wasn't sure this was right, but rather than consult Doctor Resnick, he composed a letter to her.

The next letter was from a woman whose son had just been arrested for hitting a policeman. Max did not want to think about it. He tried another letter, but he found he could not make any more decisions. Suddenly he picked up the remaining letters and dumped them on Shmuel's desk. "Finish for me, Shmuel," and he went out. He saw the receptionist look at the clock as he passed her desk, but he did not stop until he was at Clara's door.

"I have to talk to you," he said to Clara, who stood in the doorway, wiping her hands on her apron.

154

"Come in," she said, but she sniffed at him before she turned and went into the living room and Max, following her in, said, "I'm not drunk."

Arnold was sprawled on the couch reading a book.

"Go do your homework," Clara said.

"What homework?" Arnold asked, but Clara was pushing him into the bedroom.

Max sat on the easy chair by the window. He wanted to tell her about Holtz, but he couldn't do it and when she took a seat opposite him and composed herself, hands folded in her lap, he was nearly as surprised as she was to hear himself say: "Clara, will you marry me?"

For minutes the only sound was from Arnold in the bedroom. Clara wiped her hands on her apron, getting the flour she had rubbed off back on her hands. Max wondered if he should fall on his knees and ask again or if he should take it back. Only her silence told him she heard what he said. Finally she stopped wiping her hands and stood up. "You're coming tomorrow night, Max. Let me think about it until then."

"Don't think," Max shouted. "Tell me now!"

She shrugged her shoulders. "A woman likes time to think. Even if it's only a formality."

Max stood up. He looked out the window and saw the evening fog gathering by the street light. Yes, he thought, it is only a formality. "That's all right," he said.

"Do you want to stay for dinner?" Clara asked.

"No," Max said. "I have to go somewhere."

He was out of the house before she could ask another question and on Geary Boulevard he hailed a taxi. "The Hall of Justice," he told the driver.

In a few minutes he was there. He pushed through the crowds leaving the Hall and gained the marble lobby out of breath. There was only one man at the information desk. Max went to him. The officer wore a blue business suit. "Are you a policeman?" Max asked.

The officer's eyes narrowed. "Yes."

"I killed Linda Jordan."

"What?"

"I killed Linda Jordan."

18

Max sat alone in a pleasant office on the fourth floor of the Hall of Justice. The patrolman who led him there was posted outside the door. Every once in a while Max could hear him speaking to someone in the hall, but he never seemed to say anything about Max being in the office and Max began to wonder how long he would have to wait. He got up and tiptoed around the room. Besides the desk there was an old couch, two straightback chairs, and a row of filing cabinets. Behind the desk was a leather chair that tipped back and pointed to the window. Max looked out at the lights outlining the hills to the south; he tried to imagine himself looking out through bars, waiting for the guards to come and lead him to the execution chamber.

Someone was at the door. Max felt his heart turn to ice and then melt again as the patrolman's voice said, "He's inside." Max sat down quickly, wondering if he would be given the third degree.

A man came and stood in the open doorway. He wasn't wearing a uniform. Max smiled politely. Finally the man seemed to make up his mind. He came into the room and seated himself at the desk. For a minute they just stared at each other, then the man switched on the desk lamp and said, "Now, what's all this about you killing the Jordan girl?"

Max didn't know what to say. He thought he made it clear to the officer at the information desk who ran his hands up and down Max's body and then, satisfied that Max did not have a gun, marched him up to the fourth floor. There the officer told the desk sergeant what Max had said and Max repeated it himself.

"Are you a policeman?" he asked.

"Lieutenant Sloane. Homicide." He said it quickly, a man used to identifying himself, and then he leaned back in his chair and pressed his fingers together. Lieutenant Sloane was a big man; when he leaned back the chair disappeared behind him and he seemed to be leaning on air. A gray suit just barely managed to cling to him and a bright red tie flapped outside the jacket as if there were not room for it inside. He leaned forward suddenly and slapped the table. "You didn't kill the Jordan girl," he said. He wasn't asking anything; he was announcing his decision. For a minute, Max was afraid the lieutenant was going to leave and that was all there was to it, that he had somehow been seen through and would soon be tossed out of the police station as an imposter. He avoided the detective's eyes.

"Do you read the papers?" Sloane asked.

"Yes," Max said. Then he added, "Sometimes."

"Do you know a man was found guilty yesterday of killing that girl?"

"Yes, of course. That's why I'm here."

The detective got up and paced around the room. He stopped at the files and drummed his fingers on them, then came back to the desk and sat down again, leaning across the desk and pointing a finger at Max. "How old are you?"

Max had stopped counting the years, had even lost the

habit of noting his birthday in the camp when one often did not know what day it was. "Fifty-seven," he said, calculating quickly. "No, fifty-eight."

"What do you do?"

Max described his job, wondering what it had to do with his confession. He had not slept well the night before and now his stomach reminded him that he forgot to eat dinner. When he finished telling about the agency he yawned and apologized.

"Where were you born?"

"Berlin."

"You're Jewish, aren't you?"

Max nodded. He thought of repeating his confession. "I don't-" he began, but Lieutenant Sloane began to speak at the same time. They both stopped and Sloane suddenly whirled in his chair and looked out the window. Max saw that the man worked in sudden motions, as if he were the victim of a constant series of inspirations, and he waited for him to jump up. He was not disappointed. Lieutenant Sloane leaped from his chair and in three strides was at the door. "I'll be back," he said.

It was getting late and Max's eyes were growing heavy and searching for sleep. He wondered why they couldn't question him in the morning, or why they had to question him at all since he had confessed. His eyes closed and soon he thought he heard Clara outside his room. She was asking if she could come in. The door opened and Max woke up. Lieutenant Sloane was back with another man. Sloane sat at the desk and the other man, also dressed in plain clothes, but more slightly built with a fringe of brown hair and a pencil-stripe moustache under his hooked nose, seated himself on top of the desk. "This is Lieutenant Jacobs," Sloane said.

"How do you do," Max said, wrinkling his forehead to

hold his eyes open.

Lieutenant Jacobs leaned close to him. "Why do you want to make trouble?" he asked confidentially.

"Trouble?" Max shook the sleep from his head. "What do you mean trouble?"

"The man who killed Linda Jordan is named Holtz. We had a long investigation, there was a fair trial, and yesterday twelve impartial citizens found him guilty."

"You don't understand."

"I understand," Jacobs said. He spoke very slowly and patiently, like a teacher addressing a backward pupil. "Every time there's a murder three or four people come down here and confess. They can't all be guilty. Am I right?" He waited for Max to answer, but it was a moment before Max realized an answer was expected. "Yes," he said. "I guess so." "Not you guess so," Jacobs said. "You know so. They can't all be guilty and you can bet that none of them are guilty. You know what's wrong with them? Some of them are feeling guilty they weren't kind to their mothers and they want to confess to killing somebody so we should punish them. Some of them just want to be famous. They want to sit up there in the witness box without actually having murdered anyone. You're very tired, aren't you, Max?" Jacobs nodded his head. Max, surprised to hear his name, nodded with the detective. "Why don't you go home and get some sleep," Jacobs said, "and forget all about this killing and raping." He nodded his head, but Max held his head still and said in a loud voice: "I killed Linda Jordan."

Lieutenant Sloane, who had carefully studied his fingernails while Jacobs spoke, jumped out of his chair. "Now look here, Friedman," he yelled. Jacobs grabbed his arm and pulled him to the side of the room where they whispered to each other. Sloane's outbreak cleared the air of the fog that Jacob's soft voice had produced and Max was tired but fully awake now. He watched the two detectives huddle together and he knew they were plotting to take away from him the decision he had made. When they came towards him again, Max stood up to meet them.

"I'll tell you what," Jacobs said. "We're going to go now. We got other things we have to do. Anytime you change your mind, you're free to leave. You can go right out that door and go home and get a good night's sleep."

"Suppose I don't change my mind?" Max asked.

"This is a serious matter," Sloane said.

"Yes," Max replied softly, catching Jacobs' tone. "I know it's serious."

Sloane was about to say something else, but Jacobs pushed him towards the door. Over his shoulder Jacobs said, "Think about it." They walked out, leaving the door open.

Max sat in the chair. Sloane had left the desk lamp on and the light hurt his eyes so he got up and turned the lamp off. Then he sat in the chair again and held his head in his hands until he fell asleep.

When he woke up he thought at first it was morning and he was in his own room in the Richmond. Wondering why it was still dark, he searched for his clock, but there was no ticking sound and he realized now as the unfamiliar shapes in the detective's office established themselves, there had been no alarm. What am I doing here? he asked himself. Then he remembered where he was and what he had done. He turned on the desk lamp and looked for Sloane or Jacobs, but there was no one there. His own watch had stopped and he did not know what to do. The door was still open. *Must I go through with this*? He thought of leaving. What business was it of his if a Nazi waited to die for a crime he had not committed? Wasn't that the way the world went? He got up and took a step towards the door. He had his own life to live, and he thought of Clara and smelled the rich oily odor of her cooking. Max stepped out into the corridor Two men hurried by; they did not pay any attention to him. At the end of the corridor the desk sergeant watched him for a minute and then returned to his book. He was free to leave. He took a step down the corridor and looked back at the desk sergeant. He took another step and his eye was caught by a display of wanted posters. Some of the pictures had numbers hung around the necks of the criminals. Max had seen such pictures in the post office, but he never thought about them before. Now he rolled back his sleeve and looked at his own number. He took another step and stopped again. Four policemen came in together, their boots tramping time in the marble hallway. *Wo gehen wir hin?* Sarah's laughter rang in his head and he turned back and asked the desk sergeant for Lieutenant Jacobs.

"He's off duty now," the desk sergeant said. "Can I help you?"

Max was staring at the intricate buttons on the sergeant's uniform. "Call him please," he said. "It's important."

In half an hour, Lieutenant Jacobs arrived at the station. Max was seated on a bench where he had watched a drunk being brought in, supported by two policemen, and then a woman accused of picking pockets on Market Street. "You got a cigarette, Honey?" she asked Max, but the officers led her off before Max could answer. Then Jacobs arrived. "What's the matter with you?" he asked. "I was just about to go to sleep."

"I can prove that I killed the girl," Max said. "I didn't mean to, but I did." He took his keys out of his pocket and handed them to the detective. "In the top drawer of my bureau you'll find a button from the girl's dress. I tore it off when we fought."

Jacobs tossed the key in his hand. "I don't want to believe you," he said.

"I know," Max said. "I'm sorry."

For a moment their eyes met and then they both turned away. "Go quickly," Max said. Tears were swelling in his eyes.

The detective started walking towards the door. He was still tossing the key.

"My address is-"

"We know what your address is," Lieutenant Jacobs told him. Then he turned to the desk sergeant and said, "Watch this man. Read him his rights," and left the station. Max took a deep breath and moved down the bench, closer to the desk sergeant.

19

Max looked around for something to read but there was only the magazine on the sergeant's desk and he did not dare ask for that so he occupied himself by thinking of Holtz being released. He wondered when they would let him go. Perhaps even tonight someone would unlock his cell and gently shake him until he woke up. *You can go now*, they would say, *someone has confessed*. Perhaps Holtz would come to visit him and when he saw that the man who set him free was Jewish they would shake hands and Holtz would say that he was going to quit being a Nazi.

He did not realize he was asleep until a policeman poked him with his nightstick. "No sleeping here," the policeman said, and disappeared before Max could ask why.

It was cold in the station. Max stuffed his hands in his pockets and listened to the thin sound of a siren growing in the night outside. Then, an hour after Max had given him the keys, Lieutenant Jacobs returned, bursting into the station and coming down the corridor in long, stiff strides. Max stood up to meet him, but Jacobs, marching past, only shook his fist with the button in it and conferred with the desk sergeant.

Max took a few steps toward the desk. "Don't move!" the sergeant yelled at him, and Max froze in the middle of the room. The sergeant called another officer who came and led Max to a cell. When the door snapped shut and the officer locked it and went away, Jacobs came and said, "We'll see you in the morning."

"You found the button?" Max asked.

"Yes. And we talked to your landlady. She confirms that you went to the park that night. She says when you came back you looked distraught."

"That's what she said, 'distraught?'"

Jacobs looked at his notes. "Yes," he said. "Distraught." He stood there until Max said again, "I'm sorry," and Jacobs grabbed the bars in his hands and said furiously, "Shut up! Don't say another word!"

For the third time that night Max slept and in the morning he was served some oatmeal, toast and coffee and then led to an office a little larger than the one he had been in the night before. An immensely fat man with sad coweyes introduced himself as Captain Harkness. Jacobs was there too, sitting on the corner of the desk and looking as if he had not slept since Max saw him last. He held his eyes open to stay awake and they were as large as the button which sat next to him in a plastic bag on the captain's desk. Another man was also in the room, an officer busily setting up a tape recorder. Captain Harkness leaned back in his chair and hummed to himself, Jacobs fought with his eyelids, and Max looked out the window at the gray hills of the city. Finally, the officer was ready. He put a microphone in front of Max. "Say something," he said.

Max, his eye on the traffic winding down the steep street, said, "Can I make a phone call?"

Jacobs jerked his eyes open. He glanced at the Captain who was shaking his head and then he said to Max, "Last night you couldn't wait to confess and now you want your lawyer?"

"No," Max said. "I just remembered I won't be able to go to work today. I wanted to call and tell them. I already missed most of this week."

Jacobs turned to Captain Harkness again. The captain shook his head.

"I guess it doesn't matter," Max said. "I guess I won't be going back to work anymore." He sighed and slumped a little in his chair.

"Let's get on with it," Jacobs said. He looked at the patrolman who had taken a position at a typewriter table in the corner. "Are you ready?" Jacobs asked. "Ready," the patrolman answered.

Jacobs punched a button on the recorder and a spool of tape began to unwind. There was a soft hum from the machine as if it were getting ready to speak. Captain Harkness leaned over his desk. Jacobs, wrinkling his forehead to keep his eyes open, watched Max, and Max watched the machine. "Ready," the patrolman in the corner repeated. "Go on," the captain urged.

Max was remembering the time a reporter came to the Army hospital where he rested after being released from the camp. The reporter wore a suit and he brought the musky odor of cologne into the hospital with him. "What was it like in the camps?" the reporter asked, his pencil poised over his clean new notebook, and Max, ashamed to be interviewed in the pajamas the army had given him, huddled down beneath the blankets and wondered how to answer. "What was it like in the concentration camp?" the reporter asked a little louder. "*Like?*" Max said. "It wasn't like anything." The reporter made a note and then asked, "To what do you attribute your own survival?" Max thought about it for a while. Then he said: "No one survived."

"Go on," Captain Harkness repeated.

"Tell us about you and the Jordan girl," Lieutenant Jacobs said. "What happened on the night of June the third?"

The tape recorder hummed and time spun back to the present. Max moved up close to the microphone and told the machine that on the night of June third he went to the park.

"Not so close," Jacobs said, moving the microphone back an inch.

"Why did you go to the park?" Jacobs asked. Captain Harkness lit a cigarette and offered it to Max. He shook his head and Harkness offered it to Jacobs who also shook his head so the captain shrugged his shoulders and puffed contentedly at the cigarette himself. "Why did you go to the park?" Jacobs asked again.

"Why I went to the park? I guess I was lonely. I often go to the park at night when it isn't crowded." He stopped and watched the blue smoke reach for the ceiling.

"Then what happened?"

"Then a young girl came and sat down on the bench. She was out of breath. I guess she had been running. She sat down on the bench and I asked her if she had been running. She said she had been running and then we began to talk. The next thing I knew"

"What did you talk about?" Jacobs asked. "Do you remember?"

Max was suddenly aware that the typing had stopped. He looked at the officer in the corner, but the officer, fingers poised over the typewriter keys, did not look back. "Then I—," Max said, and stopped to listen to the typewriter click off his words and wait patiently in mid-sentence for him to continue, but he was only testing the typist and he wanted to laugh at his little joke, but instead he swallowed and went on. "We talked about the weather. She asked me where I was from, you see she noticed my accent. I asked her name. What does it matter?"

Jacobs started to say something, but the captain waved his hand and made the cigarette between his lips dance as he said, "Go on. This isn't very interesting so far."

Making up a story was an effort and Max was angry with himself because he had all night to prepare a tale and he wasted his time sleeping. "She moved closer to me," he said slowly, and then he pictured himself sitting on the bench and the girl next to him and then it was easy, he had only to describe what he saw to tell the story and join the ranks of the great authors he had studied in the university. He took a deep breath and went on confidently: "She moved closer to me and I smelled whisky on her breath. I asked her why she drank and she told me her parents did not understand her. She said her father yelled at her and made her break off going with her boyfriend and so she took a few drinks. I told her I thought girls her age should be allowed to make their own decisions and then she said she wished that I was her father."

Jacobs and Captain Harkness both leaned forward and Max told them what he saw. First he patted her on the head because he had never had a girl of his own and the next thing he knew his arm was around her and she leaned her head against his chest. "Suddenly, she kissed me. I didn't know what to do. You understand, it was thirty years since anyone kissed me. Then she suggested we go for a walk." The office itself became Golden Gate Park for him, the lamp turned into a tree and the little grove was just behind the desk. "We walked a little way and she put her arm around me. I said 'Let's go in there,' so we left the path and went into a little grove and I got excited and started to touch her in different places and she said I was a dirty old man. I slapped her and she kicked me. Friendly at first, you understand, joking, then harder. I was still touching her and then she kicked me here. In the groin. I shook her and we fought. That's when the button came off her dress. I pushed her to the ground and.and made love to her. I didn't notice that she hit her head on a bottle. When I saw the blood I got scared and went home."

"She hit her head on the bottle?" the captain said. "Then what happened to the top part of the bottle?"

Max became confused. He turned to Harold for help. "My fingerprints were on it so I threw it away. Wasn't that smart?" The tape recorder whirred like an insect. "I'm not such an old man as I look," Max added.

Captain Harkness said, "Just for the record, then, you did rape her?"

"No," Max said. He pictured the body on the ground, the skirt pulled up over the face. When he pulled the skirt down he saw Clara lying there and he bit his fist. Then he remembered what the boy had said, that no one would believe him. "The whole thing was an accident"

"A fatal accident and it was caused by you. If you didn't rape her, how come her panties were down and there was semen in her vagina?"

167

"I don't know." He felt strangled by his own lie.

"You don't know? If you confess to killing her but not to raping her, you could be put on trial for both."

"All right, there was sex. I thought she consented."

They waited another minute and then Lieutenant Jacobs leaned over and shut off the tape recorder.

The room seemed suddenly cold. Max looked to see if the window was open, but it wasn't. The sun shattered on the windowpane and seemed to close in on him. He shaded his eyes with his hands but his hands began to shake and he squeezed them between his legs and then he was rocking back and forth the way his grandfather did when he prayed. Someone came and stood next to him and Max started to scream, but it was only the officer holding a sheet of paper and trying to hand Max a pen. Clara, lying in the grove in Golden Gate Park, her throat slashed, cried out to him, *No, Max, no!* His teeth were chattering and when he raised his hand it shook so violently he could not take the pen. Lieutenant Jacobs took it instead and put it on the desk on top of the typewritten page. He motioned the officer out of the room.

"This is a confession," Lieutenant Jacobs said. "It's a copy of what you just said. Sign it when you are able to. You can read it first."

Max picked up the paper, but he could not read it for the tears in his eyes. Everything looked dim and slightly magnified as if they were all in a fishbowl, or perhaps only he was in the bowl looking out, and he wondered if that was the way things look to a fish. When he felt he could control his hand he took up the pen and signed the confession without reading it and then his eyes could no longer hold the tears and he cried.

They left him alone for a little while and then a patrolman came and he thought they would lock him up, but he was led first to a brightly lit room where they took his picture with a number hung around his chest. Another number, he thought, and before they could take it from him he turned the number around so he could see it and compare it to the number on his arm. They took his fingerprints too and then, at last, they led him to a cell.

20

You plan and you plan and when you look at your life it is a mess of loose ends. Max counted them out on the bars of his cell. There was Clara who would soon wonder why he did not call. There was the agency. What would they do when he did not show up and did not call to say he was sick? Perhaps they would send Shmuel to see what was wrong. And what would Shmuel do? He would soon have someone new to talk to. Max could see Shmuel explaining the system to the new man, introducing him to Mr. Goldman and Mrs. Kipnis. There was his apartment with his books and clothes and dishes what would happen to them? The Thompsons would watch for him on television. Perhaps if they put him on television he could say something to the Thompsons. The old man would like that. He put his fingers on another bar. Sarah! Does she approve? He looked up. Well, Sarah, what do you say? Are you proud of me? Am I a *mensch*?

Across the way was another cell and in it a man sat on the edge of the bed and studied the floor. Max pressed his face to the bars. The man across the way was dressed in a blue business suit and Max wondered how long he had been there and what, if anything, he had done. "Hello," he called. The man looked up briefly and then turned back to

169

the floor. Max put his finger on the last bar. And me? What am I doing here? He wondered if he were insane and he quickly took stock of himself, even running his hands up and down his body, but everything seemed to be in place. I don't feel insane, he thought, but how does a maniac feel? He had no desire to scream or to bang his head against the bars. Only he felt cold. In fact he was shivering just a bit, but perhaps the jail itself was cold. He wanted to ask the man in the blue suit if he was cold too, but just then an officer came to the cell across the aisle and led him away. Watching him was like watching himself and Max followed the stranger as far as he could see, wondering where he was being taken and whether they were going to take away his blue suit and give him one of stripes.

After lunch a detective came and told Max to get ready; he was going to go before a magistrate for a preliminary hearing. Max didn't know how he was supposed to get ready. "I already confessed," he said, but the detective just stood there so Max tucked in his shirt and said "I'm ready." On the way they stopped at the men's room. The detective handed Max a razor and suggested he shave and comb his hair. "There are some photographers waiting," he said. "You'll want to look pretty."

"Photographers?" Max took the razor. As he shaved he saw his face reflected not in the mirror but in the front page of the newspaper. Like a criminal, he thought.

In the press room reporters swarmed around him. Flash bulbs stung his eyes and he tried to look away, though he noticed the detective was standing very close to him and smiling. When the cameras stopped the questions began. Microphones sprouted from some of the hands before him and were held up to his face; other hands held pads and pencils. "Is it true you have confessed?" someone shouted. And then the questions came all at once. "How did you meet the Jordan girl?" "Is it true you were in a concentration camp?" "Did you know Holtz?" Max answered yes or no, trying to sort out the questions, until he realized there was really no need for him to answer at all since the reporters went on asking and writing whether he answered or not. He started to explain that to the detective when he heard a woman's voice ask: "What made you give yourself up?"

"Why did I give myself up?" he repeated. He thought he knew the answer to that when he went to Clara's house. At least, he told himself while trotting along Geary Boulevard, he would know the answer when he needed it. Then at night, while he slept in Lieutenant Sloane's office, he thought he had it, but he lost it when he woke up thinking he was home. And in his cell in the morning he decided not even to think about it because he was afraid if he thought about it too much he might change his mind. Now he needed an answer and he did not have one. "It's none of your business," he said, more irritated at himself than at her. Only as he heard his answer did he realize that the room had been still for several seconds. The detective took his arm. "That's enough, guys," he said, and led Max away. One photographer ran after them shouting, "Roll up your sleeve. Just one more picture. Will you roll up your sleeve?"

"I didn't mean that," Max shouted, looking back over his shoulder. He wanted to return to the woman reporter and apologize but the detective pushed him through a doorway and hustled him down the back way to the court.

In the audience a few people talked to each other or read newspapers until the magistrate entered and court was called to order. "You are here for an arraignment," Max was told, but he didn't pay much attention. "An

171

arrangement," he mumbled. While the magistrate told him what the charges were against him and informed him of his right to counsel, Max's eyes wandered to the front row where an old man nodded in sleep.

The magistrate and an assistant district attorney conferred and then everyone looked at Max. "I already confessed," he said. The magistrate shrugged his shoulders and the officer led him back to the little room where the detective met him and took him back to his cell.

The next day, after lunch, a guard, a friendly, grayhaired man, came to tell Max he had a visitor. On the way to the visiting room where Clara waited, the guard talked about what he would do when he retired until Max broke away and hurried to where she sat. "Fifteen minutes," the guard said.

"What are they doing to you, Max?" Clara cried, pressing her face against the partition that separated them.

"They're not doing anything to me," he said, taking a seat on his side of the table.

"I heard on the radio this morning this crazy thing. When I heard your name I fainted. I had to send Arnold out to get a paper. I thought it must be another Max Friedman, but it was your picture. I came right down, but visiting hours are only in the afternoon and I had to tell them we were engaged before they would let me see you. Even then they made an exception. Was it all right to tell them that?"

Max searched for an answer. "I'm glad you came," he said.

"I'll find a lawyer. Don't worry. We won't let them get away with this."

Max wanted to cry. She never even asked him if he did it. A real friend. He leaned his head on his fists and spoke softly to her. "Didn't it say in the paper I confessed?"

She looked up. "You confessed?"

"It must have said in the paper."

"It said, but who believes?"

"You have to believe," he said, shouting and wondering why he was shouting so much lately.

Tears started down her cheeks. While she cried, Max silently cursed Holtz and the boy both and the girl for being a whore and Golden Gate Park and San Francisco.

"We were going to be married," Clara said, shaking with tears.

Max cursed himself most of all.

"How could you do such a thing?" she said, angry for the first time. But then she shook her head and said, "No, I don't believe it."

"You must believe it," he said. "Now, go away before you get mixed up in something you don't understand." In another minute he would not be able to hold back his own tears. He looked to the guard for help and the guard understood. "Time's up," he said, taking Max away. Just before they went back through the door to the cells, Max turned and saw Clara resting her head on the table. She looked as if she were asleep. He did not envy her.

The next morning the guard announced another visitor.

"Clara?" Max asked. "The woman?"

"No," the guard said. "A lawyer."

On the way to the Attorney Room, the guard told Max about his son who was a lawyer. "He lives in Seattle now," the guard said, "or I would have asked him to take your case."

"But I don't need a lawyer," Max told him. The guard showed him into the Attorney Room where a young man waited, sitting on the edge of the table and clutching a briefcase.

"Do what he says," the guard whispered, shutting the

door.

"I'm Frank Martin, your lawyer," the young man said, getting up and pulling a chair out for Max. "You of course are Max Friedman?" Max nodded.

The lawyer took a seat across the table from Max, then suddenly got up and reached across the table to shake hands.

"Excuse me," Max said, "but I didn't ask for a lawyer. Who sent you?"

The lawyer fished a paper out of his briefcase and examined it. "Mrs. Clara Axelrod," he said, putting the paper away again when Max nodded.

They waited for each other to begin. Finally, Martin, his voice a deliberate baritone, said formally, "Anything you tell me is of course privileged. That is, I will not reveal anything you say to me without your permission so you may feel perfectly free to talk." He took off his glasses and chewed on the end. A lock of brown hair hung down over his forehead, creeping as if alive towards his eye until with a sudden jerk of his head he flipped it back where it immediately began creeping down again.

Max considered telling him that he did not need a lawyer, but Clara would be hurt so he said, "What do you want me to tell you?"

Martin put his glasses back on. "Was your confession voluntary? If you were coerced in any way we can fight it." He leaned eagerly over the table.

"No, it was voluntary," Max said, and realized that his decision was irrevocable now. The cold feeling seized him again, nailing him stiff to his chair.

"No one threatened you or told you what to say?" The cold seemed to melt, leaving Max more peaceful than he had ever been before. He held his hand in the air and marveled at how still it was.

174

"No one threatened you?" the lawyer prompted.

"No," he answered, a feeling like joy mysteriously rising in him.

Martin looked disappointed.

"I'm—." He was going to say he was sorry, but he was not sorry, somehow he was anything but sorry.

For several minutes a heavy silence hung between them. Max wondered if that was all, if he should go back to his cell. Finally, Martin opened his briefcase and took out a folder. "I've spoken to the police about your case," he said, "and I've seen the confession. In addition to the confession they now have a witness. He looked in the folder, "I believe it's your landlady who remembers that you were in the park on the night of the murder. Of course by itself that isn't much, but if you don't repudiate the confession, even her testimony is more than they need."

Good old Mrs. Thompson, Max thought. He remembered watching television with the Thompsons the night after the murder and that Mrs. Thompson asked about his being in the park. But thinking of that he also remembered Mr. Thompson slicing the air with his imaginary knife and winking obscenely. "What happens next?" he asked the lawyer.

"Next step is the preliminary hearing and then, if you insist on pleading guilty, a hearing to determine punishment. The sentence will depend on whether they find you guilty of voluntary or involuntary manslaughter. I will represent you at the hearings of course and considering your age, the fact that you have a clean record, and the circumstances of the case, I think you have a good shot at involuntary. Given the publicity, however, the D.A. could go for murder two."

Martin brushed the hair back from his forehead and smiled. Max did not know what to say so he said "Thank you."

In court on Friday the lawyer told Max the D.A. wanted voluntary manslaughter. Max nodded. He looked at the people sitting behind him. Clara was there, but he did not get a chance to talk to her. The Magistrate read the charges and asked him how he pleaded. The deputy district attorney swallowed a yawn and Max considered not answering right away in order to bring some suspense into the man's life, but he decided the poor man probably got all the suspense he needed at trials; a little more and he looked like ulcers would swallow his stomach. So he started to say that he was guilty when his eyes locked with the gray tweed eyes of his own lawyer and again Max hesitated, considering this time whether to plead not guilty after all and give Martin the trial he wanted. Just that morning Martin had advised him to recant his confession and he was thinking that a trial might be interesting at that, but then he remembered that Holtz was still in jail. Martin told him that just before the arraignment proceedings began.

"Guilty or not guilty?" the judge asked.

"Guilty, your honor." Martin told him that too. Always say "your honor" when addressing the judge. What did it hurt? Now they would take him back to his cell and a week later they would bring him to court again to hear sentence pronounced. When he confessed he did not expect all this parading back and forth from cell to court. So what's your hurry? he asked himself, reflecting that in Germany it would not have taken so long.

The Judge was speaking to the clerk and Max thought, *Perhaps now at least they will let Holtz out so he can tell everyone how rotten the Jews are. And what will that Nazi think when he learns I have confessed and saved him? But Holtz is innocent he will think I really am guilty! What do you think of those old Jews, raping innocent young*

176

Aryans? You should have let us kill him when we had him in the concentration camp. Now see what he has done!

"Come on," the guard said. His lawyer had been speaking to him. Or was it the judge? Thank God she wasn't German.

The next day Clara came to see him. "You shouldn't have come," he said, taking his seat.

"You pleaded guilty." She was not accusing him of the crime, only of his plea.

"I had to. I told you."

"I talked with the lawyer. He says as long as you don't retract the confession there's nothing we can do."

Max leaned across the table. "You shouldn't have gotten a lawyer for me, Clara. I'll pay him and tell him to forget the case."

"He's trying to help you, Max."

"The lawyer is like a little boy who finds that someone has already made a house for him out of his blocks. He doesn't care whether it's a good house or not, he only wants to build it himself. But these are my blocks, Clara, and it has to be my house."

"I'm trying to help too," she said, as if she had not heard anything he said.

"I know. I'm sorry. I mean, I can't help it."

They both sat quietly, their hands folded on the table. Max smelled pickled herring on her breath and he wanted to lean forward and kiss her. Instead, he ransacked his mind for something to say. "How is Arnold?" he said at last. She told him about Arnold, how well he was doing in school and how he didn't believe Max could have done it. "Don't laugh at me, Max. The other day I sent him out to the park to see if he couldn't find something that would prove you were innocent. All he found was a candy wrapper. I thought maybe the murderer left it, but Arnold says

177

he doesn't think so."

"Someone probably left it there yesterday. The police already searched the place. Besides, I have already confessed. Let Arnold stay home and do his homework."

"Max!"

"You must get used to the idea, Clara. I'm guilty. I did it."

There was another long pause. Clara took a little handkerchief out of her purse and wiped her eyes. "I left something with the sergeant for you," she said, her voice lower than it had been. "Just some store-bought because I didn't know if they allowed. Next time I'll bake a cake."

"I wish you wouldn't go to any trouble."

"It's no trouble." Then, leaning closer and lowering her voice still more she whispered, "Should I put a file in the cake?"

"A file in the cake?"

"To saw through the bars." She made a sawing motion with her hand. "It's a joke." She laughed a little.

"Yes," Max said. "I see." He laughed with her.

The guard tapped Clara's shoulder. "Time's up."

They said goodbye and Max saw Clara wiping her eyes with the little handkerchief as she went out the door. Then he let himself be taken back to his cell, but he wished that whatever was going to happen would happen quickly.

21

Increasingly, Max found his mind turning back to the barbed wire days of the concentration camp. One morning as he lay on his cot after breakfast, he remembered a peculiar incident: the Kommandant himself had come to the barracks with two of the guards and they dragged from his bunk a man who had been in the camp only a few days. Without a word, the two guards holding the man in a kneeling position on the floor, the Kommandant shot him through the head and the guards carried the limp body away. Afterwards, a rumor spread through the camp that the man was not a Jew at all but a Catholic priest pretending to be a Jew.

All day long Max thought about the priest and in the night he dreamed about him, waking up just as he was going to get a good look at his face. Fog drifted past the cell window. His head was splitting and perspiration dripped from his face. A guard came. Max wanted to ask for aspirin but the guard was new, a stone mountain of a man with a face painted lightly on the peak, and Max flinched and was afraid to ask for anything.

"Your lawyer's here to see you," the mountain said.

Max sent word that he had a headache and did not want to see anyone. While he was eating breakfast, the new guard returned and told Max to get ready for a trip to court.

"Are they going to sentence me?" Max asked.

"My job is to see you get to the courtroom," the guard said, "not to give no legal advice."

When Max stepped out of the cell, the guard slapped

one end of a pair of handcuffs on him, the other end already attached to his own wrist, and simply started walking. Max stumbled, was pulled a few steps, and then trotted alongside. He was given a chance to wash and shave and then he was manacled again and led to a little cell next to the courtroom. Not until someone knocked on the door did the guard unlock the handcuffs.

Max took a step into the courtroom and was paralyzed by what he saw. This looked exactly like the courtroom in which Holtz had been tried. He was led to the defense table. Martin looked up briefly and then returned to his papers. "I'm sorry," Max said to him. The lawyer shrugged. "I had a headache," Max explained. Photographers started snapping his picture and each burst of light blinded him momentarily. He turned away from the cameras and saw a flickering light in the ceiling above the judge's chair.

Max looked at the witness box, half expecting to see Holtz's arrogant face and then, turning again to face the audience, he blinked and immediately spotted Clara in a new dress with a little green hat and a veil. Next to her, Arnold stared back at him. The seats were almost all taken, but just coming in the door was his cousin Morris and as he looked around he saw Shmuel sitting with Dr. Resnick and in front of them were Mr. and Mrs. Thompson. The chatter of the audience seemed to grow louder, like a hundred typewriters all taking down his confession, and for one mad moment he thought he saw Sarah sitting in the back of the room. Everything in him tightened up and he wanted to run to her, but then he saw it was a stranger. "Sit down," his lawyer said, but Max remained standing. He was distracted by Clara who was waving at him and nudging Arnold who finally looked up and nodded. Max felt faint. Clara's mouth was moving but he couldn't hear what she said and then he saw that Shmuel was trying to say something too, but just then the judge came in and the clerk asked everyone to rise.

"What's going on?" Max whispered to his lawyer. "I thought they were just going to pass sentence. Why are all these people here?"

"The judge will pass sentence today," Martin whispered as they took their seats, "but first there is a hearing to determine punishment. I told you."

"I don't remember."

"In this case it will be largely a formality."

Max was aware of his headache again. The pain beat a broken rhythm over his right eye and he could not look back at all those people. He tried to listen to the clerk announce the hearing, but the voice seemed to come from some other world and when the assistant district attorney came over to consult with Martin, Max seemed to see them through a telescope.

The prosecutor handed Martin a paper. Martin looked it over and then showed it to Max. *On the night of June third...*, he read. He recognized his confession and curious to know what he had said he adjusted his glasses and bent closer just as Martin handed the paper back to the prosecutor who in turn took it to the judge.

Max was bored. The prosecutor was describing the crime to the judge, but Max couldn't get over the feeling that he was listening to the hearing on the radio, or over a loudspeaker suspended from a lamppost.

The shrill voice swept the streets clean in the Jewish district: "Behind this murder stands the hate filled power of our Jewish foe, a foe to whom we had done no harm, but who none the less sought to subjugate our German people and make of it its slave." Max ran from store front to store front, pursued by the voice. From a few blocks away came the cheers that punctuated Hitler's remarks and as soon as the speech was over and Max was running for his house a band struck up and Max could hear it coming towards his street. Shivering with fright, Max climbed the stairs and silently entered his house. His parents, peeking out the window, did not hear him come in and when he called out his mother jumped.

"Why do they hate us?" Max asked. "Why do they hate the Jews?"

His father, holding his mother's hand and leading her to a chair, said: "Ask your grandfather."

Max looked for his grandfather, but Mordecai had gone to the store for the last time.

Martin stood up and asked Dr. Norman Resnick to come to the stand.

"Dr. Resnick?" Max asked. "What for?"

The doctor was sworn in and then Martin, leaning with both hands on the rail of the witness box, demanded the doctor's name and profession. Resnick shifted his chair back an inch or two and identified himself as the psychiatristinchief at the agency where Max worked.

"And does Max Friedman-" Martin thrust his hand out behind him, in the general direction of the assistant district attorney "-work at that agency too?"

"Yes," Dr. Resnick replied softly. "That's what I just said."

Martin, clearly at a loss for words, stared hard at the doctor until the judge, who had been polishing his glasses, looked down, coughed, and said, "Pardon me, Mr. Martin, but this is a hearing, not a trial, and the doctor is your own witness."

"Yes," Martin said, backing away from the witness box. "Yes, of course."

Dr. Resnick then testified that Max had always been a steady worker and a stable person and Max tried to listen

182

but he heard other voices.

War es Rabinowitz?

Ich weiss nicht.

Wer gab ihm die Zange?

Ich nicht.

The Kommandant drew a knife across Max's bare chest and a thin red line appeared.

Dr. Resnick on his way back to the audience stopped to ask Max if he was all right.

Max stared blankly at him and then noticed that he was clutching his chest. He folded his hands on the table. "Yes, fine, thank you," he said.

And then Shmuel was called to testify. "How long have you known Mr. Friedman?" Martin asked after Shmuel had been sworn in.

Shmuel in his new tweed suit sat on the edge of the seat like a schoolboy kept after class. "We worked together five, maybe six years." His bony hands delivered the message and then retracted.

"You worked together for five or six years," Martin repeated. "Were you surprised when you heard that Mr. Friedman had committed this crime?"

"Surprised? I didn't believe it."

"Are you and Mr. Friedman very close?" Martin asked.

Shmuel glanced up. The flickering light caught his eye for a moment. "He was teaching me to play chess."

Martin waited, shuffled his feet, looked at the judge, and said, "I see." Shmuel nodded. "You and Mr. Friedman were both in concentration camps during the war," Martin said. "Do you feel that the brutal treatment Mr. Friedman received in those camps might help the court understand why he committed this crime?"

Max wanted to shout, but his mouth was stone.

"Yes," Shmuel answered.

"How?"

Shmuel moved forward on the chair and Martin and Max both moved as if to catch him, but he didn't fall. "I don't know," he said.

Martin turned completely around. The judge gaveled down the laughter in the courtroom and Martin advanced on Shmuel, his forefinger aimed at Shmuel's heart, but he seemed to change his mind and, his voice cracking, he asked the judge for a recess.

Max's cousin pushed his way to the railing and grabbed Max by the shoulder.

"Not now," Martin told him, taking Max by the arm.

"What is it, Morris?"

"Did you do it? I just want to know yes or no. If you didn't do it I will get the best lawyer I can find."

Max pulled his arm free and stared at his cousin. "Yes," he said. "I did it." Morris turned and Max watched him walk straight out of the courtroom. Clara was struggling to get to the front of the room now, but Martin took Max by the arm again and pulled him away.

"Your friend Shmuel was certainly no help," Martin said excitedly. "I would like you to testify."

"Testify?" Max cried, looking at the empty witness chair. "No. No, I don't want to testify." He started for the door. The bailiff stopped him.

"I tried to ask you this morning. If you won't testify for yourself I will have to call your fiancée, Clara Axelrod."

"Clara? No, don't call Clara." He stared at the door. "All right," he said. "I'll testify."

When court reconvened Martin called Max to the stand.

"Do you swear to tell the truth, the whole truth, and

nothing but the truth so help you God?" the clerk asked.

"Yes," Max answered, trying to keep his hand from touching the Bible.

Martin asked him to give a brief account of his education and his background in Germany before he came to America and he did so mechanically, telling about the University and the concentration camp and the trip to Israel and then to America out of memory, a phonograph turned on and played while he watched the spectators. He understood why Clara would be there and Shmuel and the Thompsons, but he wondered about the strangers, the old man sitting next to Clara, for instance, or the fat woman in front of Shmuel. Was she the same woman he sat next to at Holtz's trial? In the front row were seven young boys all in blue suits, waiting as if to be bar mitzvahed. Max felt that he would like to speak to them, if only he had time and knew what he wanted to say.

"Do you regret having committed this crime?" Martin asked.

"Yes, of course." His eyes searched now for what Holtz had stared at. It was the clock!

"Can you tell the court why a man like yourself would commit such a crime."

Max thought a moment. "It was an accident," he said. "I didn't mean to."

Martin's eyes pleaded with him to cooperate and Max answered with his eyes: *Why are you doing this to me?*

While Martin withdrew to the defense table to consult his notes, Max looked about the court. Before him the reporter sat, fingers poised over his machine; the empty jury box was to his left and just beyond it a water fountain. On the other side a large blackboard hung like a blank picture on the wall and next to it a calendar with July, August, and September showing. What else was there to look at

185

but the people and the clock?

Martin returned to stand in front of the witness box.

"The sex you had with the girl was consensual, was it not? That is, she agreed to have sex with you?"

"I thought so," Max said.

The lawyer studied the ceiling and then looked Max in the eye as if imploring him for help.

"Another man has already been convicted of this crime. Why did you confess?"

"It was my business." Max said.

"Your business?"

"I mean my duty." Max could almost hear Sarah's voice prompting him, feel her warm lips on his cheek.

"Did you know that the man whom your confession has set free is a Nazi?"

"I can't help that."

The courtroom had grown very still. Only Martin's voice, in tones of surrender, disturbed the peace. "But you do regret having caused her death?"

"Yes," Max said reassuringly. "Yes, of course I do."

The prosecutor called Mr. Jordan to the stand and he testified that Max had come to his house a week or so after the crime and pretended to be looking for someone who didn't live there.

Martin asked Max what that was about and Max shrugged. Even when called to the stand and asked by the prosecutor to explain his visit to the Jordan house, Max said simply, "I can't explain it."

Then the prosecutor went over the case again in a mechanical way, arguing that it wasn't an accident at all but an act of anger when the girl resisted his advances. He recommended to the judge a sentence of ten to fifteen. That created a stir in the court, but Martin reassured Max that such a recommendation was routine.

After another brief recess, Martin made a speech in which he reminded the court that Max had never been convicted of anything before and that his confession was a sign of repentance. He paraded before the judge's bench as he spoke, but occasionally he forgot and marched to the jury box, gesturing to the empty seats. "I ask the court to remember the suffering Mr. Friedman has already—ah—suffered in the concentration camps, himself a victim of Nazi oppression. Experiences such as I am about to recount might temporarily warp the judgement of any of us." He stared a moment at the judge and then went to the table and took a book from his briefcase. Max saw the title, *Nazi War Crimes*, and tried to grab Martin's arm, but Martin pulled away and Max was afraid to speak. Martin began reading descriptions of Nazi atrocities, old Jewish men compelled to dig their own graves, teenaged girls forced into prostitution, a swastika burned into the chest of an aged rabbi. Max wanted to stop him, then decided to let him go on. Finally the judge looked down and said, "Mr. Martin, I think that is quite enough." Martin, bewildered, looked from the judge to Max and then with a sigh of defeat suggested to the court that justice in this case required mercy. The judge declared a recess.

A crowd of people rushed to the front of the room, Clara leading them, but the bailiff came and took Max to the holding cell. After a while he was taken to a detention cell where he had lunch.

Martin came to see him there. "You'll get off with five to ten," Martin said. "With time off for-" Max stood up, knocking a bowl of soup to the floor. "Get out!" he shouted. "You know nothing about it! Nothing!" And to Martin's back he whispered, "Clown." He pushed the rest of his food off the table. Back in the courtroom he held his head in his hands, waiting for the judge to return. When the clerk called the court to order, Martin prompted Max to stand and then stood himself, half turned to the jury box, his back to Max. The judge sat down stiffly in his high chair and waited for the court to settle down. The lawyer pressed Max's arm, urging him to sit. Not long ago, Max remembered, the boy's life was in his hands; now his life was in the hands of the judge. He turned to look at the judge and saw that the judge had been looking at him. "Stand up," Martin whispered fiercely, and stood up himself as soon as Max was on his feet. The judge began to read from a paper he held in both his hands.

"Max Friedman, I find you guilty of voluntary manslaughter." The judge read slowly and softly so that Max had to lean forward to hear. "I sympathize with you over the inexcusable treatment you received from the Nazis, but that sympathy is washed away by your own treatment of a seventeen-year-old girl. I have tried to take into account your age, but your age should have made you wiser." A whisper began in the courtroom and the judge banged his gavel, but there was still a buzzing in Max's head and he wished only that the judge would hurry. "I have taken into account the fact that you have no previous record and are apparently not a habitual sex offender. You will not say why you returned to the girl's house, but that act suggests an unhealthy and perhaps uncontrollable curiosity. Your uncooperative attitude this morning when you were called to testify in your own behalf indicates that perhaps you do not care what happens to you. Perhaps you seek punishment for your crime and that you shall get." Max had to remind himself that he was the subject of this discourse. He had an odd inclination to just get up and walk out, and the feeling that the judge had so hypnotized everyone that he would not even be stopped. "Only your confession and perhaps what I have noted as a desire to be punished does anything to mitigate the horror of your double crime, and your confession came rather late. Your confession may represent a sincere effort at repentance. On the other hand, our young girls must be protected from the likes of you. It seems to me therefore to be entirely consistent with the demands of justice and possibly your own desires as well to sentence you to ten years imprisonment at a place to be determined by the California Department of Corrections." He rapped his gavel, but as before it brought silence, it now brought a scream that Max recognized as Clara's, and it unleashed a confusion of noise.

22

It was an ordinary bus except for the chicken wire over the windows and as it sped quietly over the Golden Gate Bridge Max was conscious of the cold handcuff that made him the iron partner of a young man who whistled as if they were all going to summer camp. Another prisoner, a black man, told him to shut up, but the boy went right on whistling and the black man appealed first to the sheriff's deputy sitting in the rear and then to the whole busload of prisoners. The boy kept whistling. Max turned in his seat to watch the city shrink until it looked no larger than a toy that he could reach out and pick up in his hand. Then the blue waters of the bay climbed suddenly to the brown hills of Marin County. A prisoner raised himself a bit and leaned his head against the window. "Look sharp when the road curves," he told everyone. "It's the last chance to see the city."

The black prisoner caught Max's eye. "Can't you make him stop whistling?"

Max shrugged his shoulders, but he wished the boy would stop. He was trying to think.

It was two days since the judge had sentenced him. Clara came to see him, but she cried through the whole visit and at the end Max told her not to come anymore. Then the lawyer came. Max apologized for yelling at him and Martin told him he understood and was working on an appeal. "Don't bother," Max said. The bus went through a tunnel and then the road curved and Max pressed his face to the window, but he missed the city. He wondered what people back there were saying about him. Clara would never believe he did it. Poor Clara. He remembered the night he first knocked on her door. When he closed his eyes he could imagine himself standing in her doorway. *Come in, Mr. Friedman.* He recalled the warm feeling as he stepped into her apartment, the smell of blintzes, her cool hands on his forehead. Even that first night he knew he would ask her to marry him. Ah, if only..if only one night a boy hadn't jumped out on the path in front of me. He wanted to go back to Clara, to lie in her arms.

"Stop whistling already!" he shouted at the boy, and to his surprise the boy stopped.

The bus turned off the highway and started down the road to the prison. "Won't be long now," someone said. "Man, I feel like I'm coming home."

Max knew what the Thompsons would say. Mrs. Thompson will tell Mr. Thompson, *I told you so*, and Mr. Thompson will swish his imaginary knife through the air as he tells the new tenant about the old tenant.

"There it is," the black man said. Max saw the huge cream colored prison against the bay. With its towers and little windows it looked like a castle along the Rhine.

The iron doors groaned and shut behind them like great cymbals and the prisoners were led to the reception room of the prison. There they were searched and then one by one they were allowed to shower under the close supervision of a guard. Max felt an old fear creep inside him at the sight of the shower. "What's the matter?" the guard said. "Ain't you ever seen a shower before?" Max turned the water on and washed the old fear away. He thought of Shmuel, pictured him at the office hurrying across the room with his little duck walk, waving a letter and saying something, but Max could not decide what. Then he remembered the night Shmuel had come to visit him, saw him rolling up his sleeve and shouting, *We were both inside!* "Hurry it up," the guard said. Well, who's inside now? Max thought, rinsing the soap off. He looked at his own numbers, soaped them over, and washed them once more. They looked a little faded to him and he started to wash them again when the guard reached in and turned off the water. "All right," the guard said, "this ain't the Turkish baths."

The prisoners all lined up and were taken to be fingerprinted and photographed again, just as they had done when he was booked, and then to the Distribution Department where he traded his clothes for jeans, a denim work shirt, a jacket, and a pair of slippers. Dressed in his new clothes and with a guard on either side, he was escorted across the big yard. A few prisoners stared at them.

When they were first led into the camp they heard music and the prisoners said to each other, See, it's not so bad, and they began to laugh and clap each other on the back. The band played "Alle die Vogel Sind Hier" and some of the new prisoners started singing. Max couldn't wait to see Sarah so he could tell her she was wrong about the camps. Perhaps she could hear the music herself. He cleared his throat to join in the chorus but just then the other voices stopped, not together but one at a time.

191

Everyone was pushing against the barbed wire fence and Max too pushed his way to the fence until he could see the main yard of the camp. The band was marching around the yard. There were three violinists and two accordion players. All the other prisoners were lined up in the yard and they all wore the striped uniforms that looked like pajamas, as if they had all been brought there in the middle of the night. The band too wore the terrible pajamas. Behind them came other prisoners pulling a wagon with a man standing on it and German guards accompanying the parade. Only the guards were smiling. "What does it mean?" Max asked the man next to him, but the man replied, "Look how thin they are!" Then everyone seemed to see the gallows at the same time as the band led the eyes of the new prisoners to it. The man on the wagon dismounted and pushed aside a guard who tried to escort him to the gallows. He mounted the box himself and put the rope around his own neck. A German with a peaked cap and medals on his chest said something which the new prisoners could not hear. The guard kicked the box out from under the condemned prisoner and Max turned away. When he looked again, the man was dangling in the air and the guards were collecting the instruments from the band.

The men were lined up in the warden's office where a guard captain told them the rules. Max did not listen. He kept thinking about Clara, probably making lunch right now. It would be nice to have lunch with her; he supposed that would never happen again. And Arnold? He will go away to college and get married. Then, one day, he will comfort his mother and tell her how lucky she was. And, who knew? Maybe she was. The guard captain finished talking and the men were marched out of the office and into the main body of the prison. First they stopped outside another steel door where a guard was seated comfortably at a desk, feet up, reading a magazine. He got up and began searching the men. Max thought of telling him that they had all been searched already downstairs, but on second thought it was probably better not to say anything. The other men did not seem to mind.

Then they were in the cell block. Tiers of cells completely surrounded an open space in the middle. It looked as if a zoo had been temporarily evacuated to a warehouse, or like circus cages piled up, waiting to be loaded on trains. Feeling sick to his stomach, Max saw arms sticking out of the cages, faces at the bars. He half expected to hear animal roars fill the hall. A guard led him to a cell.

Behind him the barred door shut with a dull metallic off-key sound. Before him was the cell. A man sat on the lower of the two bunks. He had a crewcut squaring off an oval face with a nose like a handle and eyes like two drops of tea under intense dark eyebrows. It was not an unpleasant face, but the man did not give any sign of welcome. He just sat on his bunk, sleeves rolled up almost to his shoulders. The collar of his shirt stood up too. He picked his nose and stared at Max. Besides the man and the two bunks, the upper one suspended from the wall by chains, there was a sink, a toilet, a desk that also lowered from the wall, and one barred window.

"What did you do, Pop?" the man asked.

Surely there was no need to continue the lie that brought him here. "I did nothing," Max said. Before he could explain the other man burst into laughter so hard he banged his head on the upper bunk. Still laughing he reeled to his feet. There was a pounding on the cell wall and from next door a voice asked, "What's so funny, Frank?" Frank told him and soon there was laughter up and down the row. A guard came by, running his club along the cell bars so that it made a horrible rattling sound. "What's going on?" he kept asking, stopping finally outside Max's cell where Frank told him the joke.

"Nothing?" the guard said. "That old man raped a little girl. Killed her too."

The laughter ceased, except for the man in the next cell who spoke through his bars. "You? You raped a girl?" He laughed again, but only once.

"It wasn't a little girl," Max said to his cellmate. "She was seventeen. And I didn't—"

"Can it!" Frank said. "I don't talk to dirty old men."

Routine sets in quickly in a prison. At first he was glad he hadn't heard all the rules, it lent some interest to the dull passing of time, but by the third day he knew every rule the guard had tried to tell him. He decided not to shave. All day he felt his beard to see how it was growing. He would grow a long black beard like Grandfather Mordecai's. He asked Frank about growing a beard, but got no answer.

One night, after the lights were out and before he could get to sleep, he remembered the reporter's question-what made you decide to give yourself up? He thought he knew then. He had confessed so that Holtz would not become a martyr. He saw now that it was simpler than that. Holtz was evil, but he was innocent. The boy was guilty, but he was not evil. The judge and the lawyer had talked about justice, but justice lay not in the scales, it resided rather in the woman who held them.

The next day he received a letter from Martin saying there wasn't much chance of an appeal but he could apply for parole in six years. Max wished he would come and visit. Martin was not a very good lawyer, but he cared and Max wanted to talk to someone about justice. He looked at Frank and then wrote a letter to Martin saying he would be glad for some company.

Clara will come, he told himself. Then he remembered that he told Clara not to visit him anymore. She will come anyway, he thought. He would write to her. Perhaps he would explain everything and when he got out, maybe, maybe she would still be waiting. Only he would go crazy if he did not find someone to talk with. Going to the little window he caught a glimpse of the brown hills outside shining in the setting sun. It was autumn. It was always autumn in Marin County, but now it was really autumn and soon it would be Rosh Hashonah, the Jewish New Year. Another season, he thought, another year. He wept for Sarah who was murdered one fine autumn, just before the holidays. He began to shake.

When he woke up the next morning he did not remember where he was. His first reaction was to stand by the cot and wait for the Block Chief to count him. Then he heard Frank still snoring and he was all right. He washed his face over and over with cold water. At breakfast he tried to remember the blessing for bread. *Boruch ator adonoi...Boruch ator adonoi...* He held his head in his hands and tried to squeeze the words out. Then he took off his glasses and closed his eyes. *Boruch ator adonoi....*It was no use. He pushed his meal away and cried.

"Are you all right?" the prisoner across the table asked.

They took Max to the prison hospital where his temperature and blood pressure were recorded and a doctor gave him a sedative that made him drowsy. Before he went under he said to the doctor, "Listen to me. One day in the park you are walking along minding your own business..."

"That's right," the doctor said. "You just take it easy now."

When Max woke up it was night again. A single light burned at the end of the ward where a trusty sat slumped at a desk. Max looked at the next bed. Someone lay wrapped in a blanket. "Help!" he shouted. The trusty came running. People in other beds grumbled, asked what happened. Max pointed to the bed. The trusty looked. "He's sleeping," the trusty said. "Everyone is sleeping."

"Listen," Max said, but the trusty returned to his desk. Through the bars on the door Max could see a guard come down the hall. He stopped and talked to the trusty and went away.

Hunger gnawed at Max's stomach but he did not want to bother the trusty again. Lying on his stomach he could see a corner of the sky through the barred window. Suddenly words filled him, but he had to say them to himself: One day in the park you are walking along thinking you are minding your own business when a boy jumps out on the path in front of you and suddenly your life is laid out before you in a series of choices like the path where it branches off and you do not want to choose but you have to because even standing still is a choice. Even if all the choices are bad you still have to choose and there is only one choice you have a right to make, only one life you have a right to sacrifice. Sweat dripped like tears on his face and he sat up and rocked back and forth on the cot. Something inside him was opening up. It exploded silently, like a flower blooming all at once. He could see it when he closed his eyes.

Then he heard a noise, or thought he did. The trusty did not hear it. The sound came from somewhere out in the hall and sounded like music, someone playing a flute perhaps. Max got down from his cot and went cautiously to the barred door of the prison ward. No one else was awake. Even the trusty slept, hunched over at his desk.

Max looked out between the bars, down the dimly lighted corridor as far as he could see. There was someone down there, clicking his heels together and moving from side to side. Max's heart raced in time to the music. Pressing his face into the bars, Max saw Shmuel dancing down the hallway and humming a song from the old country. "Come closer," Max said. Shmuel came up to the door and Max could smell the rich egg bread on his breath. Shmuel smiled with his yellow teeth and then Max, tears of joy streaming down his cheeks, reached through the bars and pulled Shmuel even closer and kissed him on the lips.